The Littlest Bigfoot

The Littlest Bigfoot

jennifer Weiner

ALADDIN

New York   London   Toronto   Sydney   New Delhi

This book is a work of fiction. Any references to historical events, real people, or real places are used fictitiously. Other names, characters, places, and events are products of the author's imagination, and any resemblance to actual events or places or persons, living or dead, is entirely coincidental.

SUMMER WIND
English Words by JOHNNY MERCER. Music by HENRY MAYER
© 1965 (Renewed) THE JOHNNY MERCER FOUNDATION and EDITION PRIMUS
ROLF BUDDE KG
All Rights Administered by WB MUSIC CORP.
All Rights Reserved
Used By Permission of ALFRED MUSIC

For Phoebe

The witching hour, somebody had once whispered to her, was a special moment in the middle of the night when every child and every grown-up was in a deep deep sleep, and all the dark things came out from hiding and had the world to themselves.

—ROALD DAHL, *THE BFG*

CHAPTER 1

Alice

ON A CLEAR AND SUNNY MORNING IN SEPTEMBER, a twelve-year-old girl named Alice Mayfair stood in the sunshine on the corner of Eighty-Ninth Street and Fifth Avenue in New York City and tried to disappear.

She was tall, so she slumped, curving her spine into the shape of a C and tucking her chin into her chest. She was wide, so she pulled her shoulders close together and hunched forward with her gaze focused on the ground. Her hands, big and thick as ham steaks, were jammed in her pockets as always. Her big feet were pressed so closely together that a casual observer might think she had a single large foot instead of two regular ones.

1

Her hair was the one thing that Alice couldn't subdue. Reddish blond, thick, and unruly, Alice's hair refused to behave, no matter how tightly she braided it or how many elastic bands she used to keep it in place. Living with the Mane, as she called it, was like having a three-year-old on top of her head, a little kid who refused to listen or be good, no matter what bribes she offered or what punishments she put in place.

"Behave," she would whisper each morning, working expensive styling glop through the thicket before combing it carefully and plaiting it into thick braids that fell to the middle of her back. The Mane would look fine when she left for school, but by the time she arrived at her first class, there'd be stray curls sneaking out of the elastic bands and making their way to freedom at the back of her neck and the crown of her head. By lunchtime the elastic bands would have snapped and the Mane would be a frenzy of tangled curls, foaming and frothing its way down to her waist like it was trying to climb off her body and make a break for freedom. Sometimes, in desperation, she'd tuck her hair underneath her shirt, and she'd spend the rest of the day with its springy, ticklish weight against her back.

It always felt, somehow, like the Mane was laughing at

her, whispering that there were better things to do than sit in a classroom learning how to diagram sentences or do long division. There was a big world out there, and somewhere in that world Alice could be happy, or at least meet a girl who liked her, which was Alice's fondest wish. In seven different schools, over seven entire years, Alice had failed to make even a single friend.

Alice sighed and squinted, shading her eyes from the glare of the sun as she looked up the street, then down at her luggage. A brown leather trunk, monogrammed in gold, stood at her feet. Two brown leather duffels with the same golden monogram were behind her. A pair of wheeled brown leather suitcases—one small, one large— stood at her left and her right.

"This is Quality," Alice's mother, Felicia, had said when they'd bought the luggage at Bergdorf Goodman. Alice could hear the capital Q as Felicia pronounced the word. "It will last your whole life. You'll use this luggage to go on your honeymoon." Right after she'd said the word "honeymoon," Felicia had gone quiet, maybe thinking that her bulky, clumsy, wild-haired daughter might never have a honeymoon. When Alice had asked if she could buy a purple backpack, Felicia had nodded absently, handed Alice a credit card, and started poking at her phone.

The backpack had a rainbow key chain and a green glow stick clipped to its zipper, pockets full of spare hair elastics, a pouch that held a special detangling brush, and secret compartments with stashes of treats. Alice rummaged until she'd found a butterscotch candy. As she unwrapped it she felt the first curl, one at the nape of her neck, spring free.

She sighed. A yellow school bus was pulling up to the corner. Parents were taking pictures, hugging their kids, waving, and even crying as the bus pulled away. Alice wondered how that would feel, having parents who'd wait for the bus on the first day of school and maybe even be there when the bus came back.

Alice had started her education at the Atwater School, on New York City's Upper East Side, where Felicia had gone. At Atwater the girls wore blue-and-white plaid jumpers, white shirts, blue kneesocks, and brown shoes, and they sat in spindly antique wooden chairs in small, high-ceilinged classrooms with polished hardwood floors.

In her first week of kindergarten at Atwater, Alice had broken two chairs, torn three uniforms, and wandered away from her class during a trip to the American Museum of Natural History, necessitating emergency calls to her father, Mark, who was in Tokyo at the time, and to Felicia, who was in the middle of a massage. Alice could still recall the startled look on the guard's face after he finally found her asleep around the corner from a diorama of Peking Man . . . that and the sound of her father whisper-yelling on the phone later that week, telling the headmaster that he was very lucky the Mayfairs had decided not to sue.

"Perhaps she's more of a hands-on learner," said Miss Merriweather, the educational consultant her parents had hired after that disaster.

So first grade was at the Barton Academy in a downtown New York City neighborhood, where the classrooms were painted bright colors and were full of beanbags and pets, where the kids had recess three times a day, and where they learned to knit and cook in addition to read and spell and add. Alice remembered the squish, and the squeal, when she sat on the class guinea pig. The following week she accidentally freed the class turtle. The week after that she almost impaled her teacher on a knitting needle, and she had to be hunted down and dragged out of the climbing structure on the playground every time recess ended.

"A different language!" Miss Merriweather had suggested brightly. By then Felicia had worry lines in the skin

at the corners of her eyes, and Mark had gray strands at the temples of his black hair.

During second grade at École Français, Alice came home every day with her crisp white uniform blouse stained with egg yolk or paint or ink or blood. She had trouble sitting still during her lessons and trouble remembering to speak French instead of English, and mandatory ballet class was a disaster best not spoken of. (Alice's parents agreed not to sue the École for negligence after Alice fell off the stage during a recital; the École agreed not to sue them for the injuries the school music teacher, Mademoiselle Léonie, suffered when Alice landed on top of her, not to mention the loss of their piano.)

Third grade was in Brooklyn, at an "alternative school" for gifted students. At Horizons, Alice learned that "alternative" meant "no rules" and "gifted" meant "girls with parents who think their daughters are so special that breaking Felicia's antique Chinese export ware is an expression of individuality and not a cause for punishment." Alice's parents pulled her out of Horizons after a sleepover party ended with a guest using Felicia's fancy scented candle to light Alice's bed on fire, and the culprit's mother refused to make her daughter apologize. "She was expressing herself via the medium of matches," said the chagrined mother, a performance artist who specialized in taking time-lapse videos of her underarm hair's growth.

"Boarding school!" said Miss Merriweather, who was beginning to sound a little frantic, and Alice's parents agreed with what Alice, had she been present, would have found insulting alacrity. For fourth grade, she was shipped off to Swifton, a private school in Vermont tucked into a picturesque green valley between two ski resorts. At breakfast on the first day of her second week, a girl named Muffin Van der Meer said, "Show of hands! Who likes the New Alice?" (Alice was called the New Alice because there was already an Alice in the class.) She could still picture Muffin's smirk after she'd seen that not a single hand had gone up. But Swifton wasn't a complete disaster. Alice loved skiing and sledding and racing through the snow with snowshoes or cross-country skis strapped to her feet. Her parents were angry but not entirely surprised when, in December, the headmistress called in a panic to say that they'd lost Alice during a trek through the woods. By the time Mark and Felicia had chartered a plane to Burlington, then rented an SUV for the drive to Swifton, Alice's teachers had found her, deep in the forest, in a small, crooked, but competently constructed igloo. "I'm not hurting anyone," Alice said. She suspected that

her parents would have left her, had the school's insurance policy and the state's laws not forced them to bring her home.

Fifth grade was in New York City again, at the Lytton-King School, which tried, according to its website, to "celebrate the special spirit of every child."

"They'll honor Alice's uniqueness!" Miss Merriweather had promised, as Alice's parents, looking unconvinced, held hands on the love seat. Felicia stared at her pointy-toed shoes. Mark pressed his lips together. Alice, listening from her spot in the hallway, was pretty sure that her uniqueness would, as usual, be more of a problem than a cause for celebration, but at least at Lytton-King she wouldn't have to wear a uniform. Miss Merriweather was enthusiastic—"I have high hopes, Alice!" was what she said—but even among the misfits and weirdos, in a class that included a boy named Hans, who picked his nose and ate it, and a girl named Sadie, who spoke only in Klingon, which she'd learned from *Star Trek* fan fiction, Alice was an outcast. She sat alone at every meal, she read by herself during Activity Choice Time, and whenever kids had to pick partners, she ended up working with the teacher, because nobody ever wanted to partner with her.

At home, alone in the pink-and-cream room that

had won Felicia's decorator a prize, Alice would lie on her bed, underneath its lacy canopy, or sit at her white wooden desk or in the pillowed window seat that overlooked Central Park, and try to figure out what it was about her that other kids didn't like. She knew she looked different, but that couldn't be the entire answer. In every school she'd attended, there had been girls with larger bodies or horrible breath or thick and glistening braces, girls who sprayed spittle when they talked or had little mounds of white dandruff flakes on their shoulders, and even those girls had made friends. Alice wore the same kinds of clothes, even the same uniform, as the rest of the girls. She arranged the Mane as best she could to imitate their hair, and feigned interest in the books and boy bands they liked, forcing herself to sit still and listen to their chatter, even when her body ached to move. Still, there was something about her that made them reject her, almost as soon as they'd met her. Did she smell bad? Was there something about the way her voice sounded, or the texture of her hair? Was it because her parents were rich, or was it that they weren't rich enough?

Alice had examined every bit of herself—from her toenails to the top of her head, her voice, the shape of her fingers and her forearms—trying to pinpoint the difference between herself and other girls. She'd never been able to find it, but she knew it was there. She knew every time a new group of girls looked at her, and then, sometimes before she'd even said "hello," they'd turn away, giggling and whispering.

"Be patient," said Miss Merriweather. "You will find your people."

"You're fine," said Felicia, who instead insisted that there was nothing wrong with Alice—at least, nothing that a keratin hair-straightening treatment and the right kind of clothes and a few days of a cabbage-soup-and-hot-lemon-water diet couldn't fix. Alice's granny was the only one who'd offered an actual possibility.

"Maybe they don't get your jokes," she'd suggested. This had been the previous summer, when Alice had been to visit her for an allotted week. Seven perfect days of digging for clams and floating in the clear water of Cape Cod Bay or, even better, flinging herself into the icy, bracing waves of the ocean, while her granny sat on a folding chair and watched.

"What do you mean?" asked Alice. She and Granny had blanched baby spinach, then squeezed it dry and mixed it into a dough of butter and flour and ricotta cheese and freshly grated nutmeg. Alice used two spoons to scoop the dough into little rounds; Granny dropped them into the pot of boiling salted water. In three minutes they'd be gnocchi.

Granny stared into the bubbling pot. Steam wreathed her face and her short gray hair. "Sometimes, when you've got a different way of seeing the world, it can take a while for the other kids to catch up with you," she finally said.

Alice considered that. Did she have a different way of seeing the world? Was that the problem? Or was it just that she was a big clumsy weirdo who never knew the right thing to say?

For sixth grade, it was boarding school again. "Maybe what she needs is just old-fashioned discipline," said Miss Merriweather. "A dress code and a strict schedule." The Mayfairs were dubious, but they agreed to enroll Alice at Miss Pratt's in Massachusetts, which turned out to be full of fine-boned girls with silky blond hair and ancestors who'd been on the *Mayflower*, girls who hated chunky, curly-haired, freckle-faced Alice before she even opened her mouth.

Alice broke her bunk bed when she tried to wedge her trunk underneath it. She crushed her English teacher's glasses by accidentally sitting on them during her first Shakespeare class, then tried to run away after her roommate Miranda left her diary on the common room couch, opened to a page that read, in all capital letters,

"ALICE IS ANNOYING AND UGLY AND DRIVING EVERYONE NUTS."

In January she was asked to leave after she stole another girl's care package and ate all of the cookies it contained.

"I was so hungry," Alice said, in her smallest voice, in the backseat of her parents' Town Car, which they had sent to pick her up. Lee, the driver, looked back at her, his expression sympathetic.

"Bad food?" he asked.

"The worst!" said Alice, and she told him about the lumpy oatmeal for breakfast and the endless iceberg-lettuce salads for lunch. "Stealing those cookies," she said, "was an act of survival. Besides, it wasn't like Carter was going to eat them. She was on a diet. They were all on diets." She shuddered. Alice loved food—cooking it, eating it, looking at cookbooks and food-centered magazines, reading reviews of restaurants she wanted to visit someday. She hadn't done well in a place where her classmates considered salad dressing a special treat.

Alice was positive that her new school, Lucky Number Eight, would probably be just as bad as the seven that had preceded it, even though it looked different from the rest of them.

The Experimental Center for Love and Learning, a boarding school in upstate New York, where Alice was headed this September morning, had been open for only four years and had moved to its current location over the summer. Most of the links on its website led to pages that said "UNDER CONSTRUCTION!" with a smiley face wearing a hard hat floating above a cartoon hammer and saw. There were shots of one big log-cabin building called the Lodge, which held the dining hall and classrooms. The dorms looked like the rickety ice-fishing shacks that Alice had seen during her winter in Vermont . . . but the lake, and the forest, looked pretty.

"It's an open environment. It's a working farm, so the children can learn about the world in a really hands-on way," Miss Merriweather had told her, before reaching over to give Alice's hand a squeeze. Dimples flashed in her cheeks when she said, "I have a good feeling about this one," and Alice found herself smiling back before she ducked her head, remembering that her teeth, like everything else about her, were too big . . . and that Miss Merriweather had also had a good feeling about Alice's seven previous schools.

"We'll miss you, kiddo," her father had said to her that morning. In a T-shirt and pajama bottoms, Mark was long-limbed and lanky, and in his suits he looked as solid and substantial as a wall, with thick black hair neatly combed, polished black shoes, and that morning, a silky tie the deep bluish-purple of a bruise. He brushed the top of her head with his lips, his *Wall Street Journal* tucked under his arm, an iPad in one hand, and an iPhone—one of three he used—in the other. "We'll see you for Christmas."

Alice stood in his dressing room, surrounded by his suits, wishing he'd stayed longer or said "I love you" before he left. She wished she could hide against the wall, concealed by hanging jackets, the way she had when she was a little girl. She'd wiggle the suits, making them talk in squeaky voices, while her father pretended that he didn't know she was there and asked the suits if they'd seen her.

Instead, after saying good-bye to her father, Alice had straightened her shoulders ("Don't hunch!" she heard Felicia scolding in her head) and made her way toward her mother. Felicia's dressing room was lit by lamps lined with pink satin—because, she'd once told Alice, that was the most flattering light for a woman's skin. It smelled like Chloé perfume, hairspray, and the secret cigarettes that Felicia occasionally smoked, and it looked like a dollhouse, with the furnishings and the clothes all slightly smaller than what a regular-size person would require. It was where, when Alice was five years old, her mother had said, "I'd like it if you could call me Felicia instead of Mommy." Her mother's red lips had curved into a smile. "It makes it sound more like we're friends, you know?"

You'd never pick me to be your friend, Alice thought but did not say.

She stood and watched as Felicia, elegant before her mirror, used tweezers to painstakingly glue individual fake eyelashes to her real lashes, then tilted the perfect oval of her face, with its high cheekbones and elegantly arched brows, this way and that.

"How'd you sleep, baby?" Felicia finally asked.

"Fine," Alice lied. She'd had one of her strange not-quite-nightmares again, but she knew, from experience, not to bother Felicia about that.

"I'd take you up to the school myself," Felicia murmured as she painted her mouth with a tiny brush she'd dipped into a pot of bloodred gloss, "but I've got a meeting."

Alice nodded. Her mother didn't work, but her volunteering was practically a full-time job. Diabetes on Mondays, Crohn's disease on Tuesdays, cancer on Wednesdays, and heart disease on Fridays, with Thursdays reserved for the hair salon, mani-pedis, and Pilates lessons.

Felicia got to her feet, put her slender arms around Alice's shoulders, and pressed her cool, powdery cheek to the top of Alice's head, all the while keeping her body angled away from her daughter's. *As if I'm catching,* Alice thought, wondering, for the thousandth time, how she could have ever emerged from this slim and perfect woman, and wondering why it was so hard for her to leave.

No one here wanted her. She was an impediment, an embarrassment, an unwanted gift that had arrived without receipt and couldn't be returned. Her parents would shove her under a bunk bed if they thought that no one would notice she was gone. Maybe it was just that at home she knew exactly what kind of awful to expect, whereas each school was a revelation, a new adventure in misery and isolation.

Alice knew her mother's dream: that one year she'd come home from school transformed into the kind of slender, smiling, appropriate girl they could have loved. So far it hadn't happened. As much as Alice wanted to please her parents—to see her father look happy, to make Felicia's painted lips curve into a smile—she also wanted to run in the sunshine, to play in the dirt or the mud puddles or the snow, to eat the warm chocolate chip cookies that her Granny baked during her visit every summer, and to ruin her shoes by letting the waves wash over her feet. As hard as she tried, Alice could never stop being herself. She could never make herself be the kind of girl they'd love.

Standing on the corner, sweating in the late-summer heat, still feeling the cool imprint of Felicia's cheek on her head, Alice kicked at the corner of the monogrammed trunk and shut her eyes, listening for the sound of her parents' car. A battered white van cruised slowly down the street, then backed into an illegal parking spot and sat there with its flashers on.

Alice rummaged in her bag for another butterscotch and wondered why her parents kept hiring Miss Merriweather, who'd been wrong about seven different schools in a row. She wondered too whether her new school, the Experimental Center, was as weird as it sounded in the letter the school had sent to parents, which began:

We humbly acknowledge the profound act of surrender it will be to entrust to us your INCREDIBLE YOUNG HUMANS, the most unspeakably precious beings in the world. It's an honor we take with the utmost gravity, that we are part of the village that will raise them. We will strive to teach the values of honesty, integrity, and respect for themselves and the world to your daughters, your sons, and your non-gender-conforming offspring. We promise an atmosphere of inclusivity and respect, where hierarchies are nonexistent, where age and grades don't matter as much as the understanding that we all have things to learn from one another.

Alice shook her head, thinking that getting rid of her every September was not an act of profound surrender for her parents, but one of great relief. *And what could anyone learn from me?* she wondered. How to break combs with your hair? How to outgrow your entire wardrobe every three months? How to make your mother cry by spilling grape juice on her new suede boots, and then shrink her favorite white cashmere dress in the dryer until it was too small for even a Barbie doll because you couldn't bring yourself to tell her that you'd gotten juice on that, too?

Alice closed her eyes, testing herself. She could hear the wheeze of a city bus as it heaved itself around the corner, a taxicab that needed a new muffler, one of those electric cars that barely made a sound. No Lee, though. She smiled, remembering how Lee hadn't believed her when she told him that she could always hear his car, specifically; how he'd made her stand on the sidewalk, blindfolded (with his wife watching) while he circled the block. Five times he'd driven past Alice, surrounded by taxis and buses and motorcycles and even other Town Cars like his, and every time Alice was able to pick out his car as it went by.

That morning, Alice waited patiently, eyes closed, until she heard the car whispering up to the curb.

"Ready to go, Allie-cat?" Lee asked. The trunk's lid popped open, and he started hoisting her luggage off the sidewalk.

Alice tried to help. Lee waved her away, saying, the way he always did, "You know I need my exercise," and then, as always, shrugging as she lifted her suitcase, then her duffel bag, saying, in a gruff Russian accent, "Alice is strong like a bull!"

Alice hated it when other kids teased her about her size, her strength, her weird wide face and untamable hair, but Lee could say anything he wanted, because Lee was safe, and nice, and would never hurt her. Every Christmas, Lee gave her a bag of Hershey's Kisses, wrapped in red and green foil. On her birthday he always sent a card, and at Swifton he'd mail care packages with Kit Kat bars and postcards of the Statue of Liberty or Central Park.

Alice climbed into the backseat—in spite of her pleading and pointing out that she was more than big enough, Lee never let her sit up front—and buckled her seat belt as Lee pulled away from the curb, heading downtown.

"Allie-cat," he began. Alice smiled, the way she always did at the nickname that only Lee used. "I understand that this place sounds a bit . . ."

"Ridiculous?" asked Alice. "Bizarre? Possibly illegal?"

"Precious," Lee said, easing to a stop at a red light. "But you need to keep an open mind."

In the backseat, Alice leaned her forehead against the cool pane of glass. Her eyes slipped shut, which was good, because then she didn't have to see herself—the parts that were too thick, too soft, too big, too round. As the car sped along the highway she slipped into her favorite daydream: of how somewhere, there were two people, a man as big and strong as the tallest basketball player and a lady whose body was as soft and warm and welcoming as her granny's when she'd let Alice sit on her lap. They were her real parents, who had been separated from her somehow, and in Alice's daydream they would run to her, crying, and they would scoop her up into their arms and hold her tight and tell her that now that they had found her, they would love her forever and never let her go.

CHAPTER 2

Millie

ON A WARM SEPTEMBER NIGHT, A GIRL NAMED Millie Maximus, wearing her favorite blue dress, climbed to the sturdiest branch of the Lookout Tree and hid herself in the shadows. It was late; the rest of the littlies were tucked up in bed, but Millie was too excited to fall asleep even if she'd wanted to.

Millie held her breath as the Elders crept out of their underground houses and came to stand around the flames. They linked their hands and bent their heads, and Millie's father began the chant. Maximus's voice was low and quiet and rumbly, like water tumbling over stones.

"I am Maximus of the Yare. Would you listen?" her father began.

"We will listen," came the response.

"We are the Yare. We are the hidden ones."

We are the Yare, repeated the men, their voices deep and soft. *We are the hidden ones.*

"We live in the shadows. We protect the silence. We guard the secret spaces of the world." Millie's mother, Septima, spoke those words, in a voice as high and piping as birdsong.

We live in the shadows. We protect the silence. We guard the secret spaces of the world, echoed the other women in their own twittery voices.

"We are the forgotten. We are the unseen. We are the guides," said Maximus. Then, as one, the Tribe chanted, "We are the Yare, and we survive." With their heads bowed, holding each other's hands, the Tribe stood for a moment in reverent silence, before they closed with a final, solemn "Nyebbeh," a word that could mean anything from "hello" to "love" or "peace" or "not right now," when said to a friend or a loved one. Millie held perfectly still, gazing down at the two dozen Elders she'd known her entire life.

Maximus stretched out his arm, poking the tip of a long branch into the fire. Once it had caught, the meeting would begin, and whoever held the stick could speak.

Maximus was the Leader of the Yare, a tribe of what humans called Bigfoots. When he Passed—"may the day be long-and-long," Millie whispered—as her parents' only child, she'd be the one in charge, bound by the traditions that had ruled her life and her parents' lives and their parents' lives and the lives of every member of every Tribe that had come before her. She would live her whole life in the forest, hidden away from the No-Furs, which was what the Yare called humans; and the most she could ever dream of doing was introducing a new strain of pumpkin or coming up with a new recipe for bread; and the closest she would ever come to the human world was watching Old Aunt Yetta's TV tapes or listening to the sound of singing when it carried across the water.

The Yare did not sing. They did not yell or hum or raise their voices. They kept quiet, they moved quickly, they blended into the forest, they faded into the background, because these were the behaviors that had kept the Yare safe from human discovery for the past five hundred years. Even their animals were quiet: Millie's little gray kitten Georgina's purrs were barely audible, and Old Aunt Yetta's goat, Esmerelda, hardly ever bleated, not even when Millie was late to milk her. That was the way it had always been, the way it would always be, and Millie was powerless to change it. It made her furious just thinking about it. "Fyeh," she muttered in disgust . . . but she muttered it very quietly.

"We all know what's happened," Maximus said in his quiet rumble, as the Speaking Stick flared above his head. "The No-Furs have built twelve new buildings . . . and this morning there was a 'Welcome, New Learners' banner hanging from two trees."

"A school," whispered Aelia. "A school means children. Children are curious. They will be having canoes or those yak-boats."

Kayaks, thought Millie, and rolled her eyes.

"They'll dare each other to come across the lake, or they'll hear us or see us, and they'll find us." Aelia began twisting her hands in her apron, and Septima was anxiously nibbling at the fur on her fingers.

Millie, meanwhile, was so giddy with delight it was all she could do to keep from dancing on her branch. A school! Maybe there would be No-Fur girls her age, and she'd be able to hear them—their conversations, maybe even their music. Maybe, maybe someday, she could find some sort of disguise or even a potion to make her fur disappear. She'd long suspected that there was such a thing, to be used in cases when the Yare absolutely had to venture into the No-Fur world. She'd figure it out and she'd make her way across the lake in a canoe or in a kayak. She'd pretend to be a lost camper who'd wandered away from her parents, and she'd meet a girl, and make up a friend, and the girl would hear Millie sing and say, "You are totally amazelling"—"amazelling" was the highest praise a Yare could get—and take Millie to the principal, who would know a ProDucer (as opposed to an amateur one), and then Millie would be where she'd always wanted to be—standing on a stage, in a shimmery silvery dress, holding a microphone, singing, while people listened to her, entranced.

Of all the Yare she knew, Millie was the only one who had such dreams, the only one who wasn't terrified of humans, the only one who'd never entirely believed the stories that the Yare littlies were told.

There was, for example, the tale of the terrible old No-Fur who had a white beard and wore a red suit that was trimmed with the fur of tiny baby Yare. Each winter he would slip down the chimneys of unsuspecting Yare families (he was so small and slender that he could, of course, easily fit). Once he'd gained entry, he would creep around the house piling food and toys and goodies into an enchanted sack that could hold an entire household's worth of belongings. He would magic himself back up the chimney, then fly away and give everything he'd stolen from the

Yare to greedy little No-Fur children, who would eat up the candy and break all the toys. "So be good," the Yare would say each winter, "or the Bad Red-Suit No-Fur will come down the chimney and be having your toys in his sack!"

Another story—even more terrible—claimed there was a No-Fur as small as a speck of sand with wings and a little white dress, so tiny that she was almost invisible and could fit through mesh window screens. This horrible creature would fly into the bedrooms of young Yare and scoop up any coins or shells or pebbles or small toys they might have left lying around their bedrooms. Then she'd slip inside of their mouths and yank out one of their teeth as punishment for not putting their things away. "So be good," the Yare would whisper, "or the Bad Fairytooth No-Fur will come through your window and be having your toys and your teeth!"

Every spring, said the Yare, the Neaster Bunny No-Fur would come hopping through the fields, pretending, for reasons that were never clear, to be a large rabbit, leaving exploding painted egg-shaped bombs hidden in the grass and stealing all the candy in the village. (Almost every Yare had a sweet tooth, so this story was especially scary to the littlies.)

And every summer on the Fourth of July, the No-Furs would celebrate a holiday they called the Banishment of the Bigfoots, with terrifying and noisy displays of fireworks that would shatter the peace of the summer evening as the No-Furs roared their approval and drank beer, and honked their car horns at one another.

Down below, the meeting continued.

"Could be it's not a school," a Yare named Marten was saying. "Could be it's another camping-ground."

"The sign said 'Learners,'" Aelia hissed.

"So a learning campground," said Marten. "Where they send the littlies to learn about camping."

"I saw targets." Aelia sounded like she was about to cry. "Targets for learning to shoot at us. That's what they're learning."

Millie shook her head, thinking it was much more likely that the targets were for archery and not Yare-hunting.

No-Furs are dangerous, was what little Yare learned . . . but Millie had never believed it. She didn't believe a grown No-Fur could fit down a chimney or fly through a window or go hopping around a meadow dressed in white fur without anyone noticing. Besides, what would No-Fur children want with Yare toys, which were all handmade, carved from wood or sewn from scraps of cloth? She had seen TV shows on Old Aunt Yetta's laptop—or "top-lap," as it was known to the Yare—and sometimes they included commercials. She knew that No-Fur children had electronic games and

flying scooters and keyboards and microphones and parents who'd listen when they said they wanted to be singers, not just stay stuck in the woods for the rest of their lives.

Millie kicked at the tree trunk, feeling familiar frustration rising. Septima glanced up, her brown eyes narrowed, and Millie shrank back, hiding herself in the shadows. "Sorry," she whispered, and patted the Lookout Tree by way of apology.

"Could be it's temporary," said Darrius, whose youngest son, Frederee, had just had his barnitzvah ceremony, officially becoming an Elder. "Maybe they'll only be there for the fall—like a campout, you see—and then they'll be going back to where they were."

Yare voices rose in a babble of squeaks and whispers. Maximus reclaimed the Speaking Stick. "One at a time," he murmured, lifting and lowering his free hand in a gesture Millie knew all too well, a motion that meant "be quiet."

Melissandra yanked the stick out of his hand. "Why are we waiting?" she demanded, without bothering to lower her voice. "They're too close. It's too risky. We should be packing already. We should be far-and-far away by now!"

"I cannot leave my garden," said Old Aunt Yetta. "My mother, and her mother before her, spent their lives on that garden. Even if I took cuttings, it would be long-and-long before I could be growing what we need."

Just as every clan had a Leader, each clan had a Healer, who managed the supply of herbs and barks and leaves, and each clan had a Watcher, a Yare tasked with keeping track of news of the No-Fur world. In Millie's Tribe, Old Aunt Yetta was both Healer and Watcher. She kept the Tribe's single top-lap computer, and an ancient television set, on which she watched the nightly news shows. Millie knew, from careful questioning, that the Yare got on-the-line with the help of something called Why-fie Modem. They got electricity by hooking into the outlets of an old campground. A single extension cord buried in the ground powered the whole village—and something called a "shell corporation" paid the bills.

All of that was known to the rest of the clan, but what the other Yare didn't know was that Old Aunt Yetta sometimes enjoyed watching more entertaining options than just news . . . and sometimes Millie watched with her. They were both partial to a program called *Friends*, about attractive young No-Furs in New York City. But Millie's absolute favorite show was called *The Next Stage*, where regular, not famous No-Furs sang or danced or did gymnastic tricks and tried to win a million dollars.

"And our buildings!" said Laurentius, a young Yare

whose voice still wobbled and cracked when he spoke. "The new lodge . . . the pens for the goats . . . we'd be needing to start all over."

The Yare village was mostly underground, a series of burrows and warrens and tunnels dug into the hillside. Everything aboveground was carefully camouflaged with panels of leaves and branches attached to pulleys that would come down and disguise doors and pens and windows with a single tug.

"So we stay here and wait for them to find us?" This time Melissandra didn't even bother trying for the stick. "Those children will be trying to come over here. And our littlies will be wanting to go over there." She glared at Maximus and Septima. "Or, at least, one of them will."

Millie hung her head as her mother huddled into Maximus's side, hands working at her apron. Maximus's voice was calm when he said, "Our Little Bit will do as she's told."

"Do as she's told?" hissed Melissandra. "Nyebbeh! How many times has she run to away? How many times has she almost been discovered? How many times will you let her be putting all of our lives at risk before you do something?" Melissandra's eyes were wild, her fur bristling on top of her head and hands and shoulders.

Millie tucked herself in even closer to the tree trunk.

She didn't want to think about the times she'd slipped away from her parents, in the forest or down by the water, drawn by the sound of No-Fur voices or just the knowledge that they were near.

"Let's not be losing our heads," Maximus said in his soothing rumble. "There are measures we can take without abandoning the village. We can cancel Halloweening."

Millie bit her lip, hard, before she could yell "No!" and give herself away. Halloween was the one time of year that the Yare were allowed to venture out into the No-Fur world. Maximus was the one who had started the tradition, after years of Millie begging and pleading and—yes—running to away.

For the last six years, each September, Maximus would pick out a town within a fifty-mile drive of the village and scout it carefully, making sure there'd be enough children in costume that a half dozen smallish Yare wouldn't stand out. On October 31, the Yare littlies, practically vibrating with excitement, would climb into the old school bus that was kept specifically for the excursion. Maximus, disguised in a trench coat and gloves and a big, floppy straw hat, would drive them to the town and park on the outskirts, and the littlies, chaperoned by the grown-up Yare who were themselves interested in the

No-Fur world, would be given the night to trick-or-treat. The Yare Elders—most of them female—would peek into the No-Fur houses or examine the No-Fur fashions, and discuss what they'd seen. ("It's called a French manicure," or "still stainless-steel refrigerators.") The littlies would dash up and down the No-Fur streets with their pillow-cases, to join packs of human children and gather pounds of candy that they'd carry home on the bus.

Every year, unsuspecting No-Furs would remark on the excellence of the Yare costumes ("You guys look so authentic!"). Every year, puzzled No-Furs would turn to their partners, asking, "Was there some Bigfoot movie I missed?" It was heaven . . . and now it was going to be taken away. She felt tears slip out of her eyes, soaking her face-fur.

"But we won't move," Maximus said. Millie sighed in relief. "Not until we know what kind of danger this presents."

"We should be having spies!" This from Frederee, who'd forgotten to take the Speaking Stick. His parents glared at him. He whispered an apology, then took the stick, then stood in silence, realizing he had nothing else to say, before handing the stick to his father, who passed it to Old Aunt Yetta.

"Spies are not a bad idea," Old Aunt Yetta said. "We should be knowing how many of them there are. How many grown-ups and how many littlies. If it's really a school or something else, and if—"

"I'll do it!" Millie hopped down to a low branch, then jumped lightly to the ground. The Yare looked at her, wide-eyed and startled. A few of them gasped. Septima gave a shriek of dismay (a quiet shriek) while Melissandra got a smug, I-told-you-so expression on her face. Millie ignored them both, as well as the Speaking Stick, as she stepped forward into the firelight's glow.

"Please," she said. "You know I'd be the best for this. I am the littlest of the littlies. I'm knowing everything there is to know about the No-Furs. I could pretend . . . or shave my fur . . . you could dress me up . . . maybe a hat, or a bonnet or such—"

"Millietta," said Maximus, pronouncing each syllable of her full name gravely. Millie bowed her head. She didn't have the Speaking Stick, she wasn't fully grown, she wasn't even supposed to be there or have been listening . . . but she couldn't keep quiet.

"Why are we having the fear of them?" she demanded in her silvery voice, sweet and warm and clear as the tones of a triangle, or a crystal glass struck with a spoon, the voice the other Yare thought was so strange. "What have they ever done to us?"

"They kill us!" Melissandra shrilled. Millie saw that her father was nodding, probably remembering the movie he'd shown her, of a Yare, long-and-long ago, who'd been hunted and hurt by the No-Furs.

"But not these ones, Papa," Millie begged. "Maybe No-Furs other places, other times, killed Yare, but these ones haven't done anything, and maybe they never would. Maybe if they just got to know us . . ."

"Nyeh!" said Ricardan, and stomped on the ground for emphasis. "This is foolishness!"

Old Aunt Yetta was looking at Millie sadly, and Frederee, who was just a year older than she was, was staring at her with his mouth hanging open. Even Darrius, who Millie didn't think was that afraid of the No-Furs, was shaking his head.

Maximus pounded the Speaking Stick once on the packed dirt. "We will watch and wait," he declared, in a voice that let them know that the meeting was over.

As the Elders whispered a closing blessing, Millie closed her eyes, waiting to feel her father's strong arms lifting her and feel her mother snaffling at her cheek-fur and whispering in her ear, *Millie, how could you* and *Don't you know better* and, worst of all, *When you are Ruler, you will have to Set the Example, Millie, you can't keep behaving like this or wishing for what will never be.*

CHAPTER 3

Milford Carruthers
BIGFOOT HUNTER

Jeremy

W HO'S NEXT?" MISS MARCH SOUNDED BORED
as she peered over her classroom from behind her old-fashioned cat-eye glasses. Miss March had been teaching at Standish Middle School for thirty-five years. She had powdered pink skin, a cap of white curls sprayed tightly in place, and a chin that proceeded directly into her chest, with a collection of loose, pouchy flesh where her neck should have been.

Jeremy Bigelow thrust his hand into the air. The entire seventh grade groaned. Miss March's glasses flashed as she glared at them.

"Let's give Jeremy the respect he gave each of you.

Jeremy?" She waited while Jeremy, dressed in jeans and his favorite "I Want to Believe" T-shirt, made his way to the front of the classroom with a remote-control clicker in his hand.

Normally, Jeremy hated school and rarely volunteered to be called on. His brother Noah had attended Standish Middle School six years ago at the age of eight. The teachers were still talking about him: the time that Noah had found an error in the algebra textbook that the publisher had been forced to correct, the time at the statewide Model UN that he'd brokered peace in the Middle East (this while representing Sierra Leone), how he'd blown through the entire middle-school curriculum in six months and had gone on to high school before he turned ten. Noah was back home now, doing a year of independent postdoctoral research before returning to MIT, which meant that Jeremy shared the house with him and their older brother, Ben, a senior at Standish High. Ben was captain of the football team, the baseball team, and the lacrosse team, an all-state player in all three sports. His bedroom wall was papered with letters from coaches from all over the country, begging him to play for them, and letters from professional football, baseball, and lacrosse coaches, importuning him to skip college completely and go pro.

Jeremy had narrow shoulders and dark-brown hair

that was always too long, because his mother usually forgot to bring him to get it cut. He was desperately uncoordinated, lacking both speed and endurance, and most sports bored him, whether he was a spectator or a participant. Academically speaking, he was absolutely average, equally uninterested in every subject.

After his brothers, it was understandable, Jeremy told himself, that his parents, Martin and Suzanne, didn't have much time or energy left for their so far unremarkable third son. They went to Jeremy's soccer games, where he was an adequate player, and signed his report cards, full of Bs and Cs, but Jeremy believed that if a stranger stopped either his mother or father on the streets of Standish and said, "Tell me about your son," they'd launch into a lavish description of Noah's research or how many goals or touchdowns or home runs Ben had scored, and it would be a long time before it occurred to either one of them to mention their youngest.

"May I have the lights off, please?" Jeremy said.

Miss March nodded at Lucy Jones, whose desk was closest to the switch. Some teachers let the kids sit in a semicircle or even on beanbags or on the floor. Not Miss March, who kept the desks in neat rows, with the troublemakers right up front.

Lucy made a face at Jeremy and flicked the room into darkness, allowing Jeremy's opening slide, red letters on a black background, to come into focus on the whiteboard.

"Bigfoots: They Walk among Us," the letters read.

The groans got louder.

"This is the exact same report he gave last year!" Lucy shouted.

Jeremy quickly clicked his remote, and the words "Now with Exciting New Research and Evidence" appeared as a subtitle. Before anyone else could complain, Jeremy began.

"As some of you may remember—"

"Yeah, from when he gave the same report last spring," whispered Olivia Núñez to her best friend, Sophie Clematis.

Jeremy ignored her. "The myth of the Bigfoot has persisted throughout time and across cultures, with sightings, illustrations, photographs, and even films contributing to the growing belief that the Bigfoot or Sasquatch, as Native Americans called them, are not merely folklore or legends but are actual beings whose existence is a closely guarded secret."

He flexed his leg muscles, then locked them to keep his knees from shaking. "Civilizations and communities, starting with the cavemen, drew pictures or told stories about gigantic, fur-covered forest dwellers. In China, they are known as the Wild Men or the Yeren. The Tlingit talk of the Kushtaka. Here in Standish, there have been reports of the Bigfoot." He clicked to the next slide. "This is a still from a nineteen sixty-seven film by Patterson and Gimlin."

He turned so that he could look at the picture of the gigantic, fur-covered, unmistakably female creature with thick arms and trunklike legs glancing shyly sideways in midstride. "This film was taken deep in the woods of Northern California by two investigators who devoted their lives to proving the Bigfoot was real."

In the back row, Austin Riley made an armpit fart.

Jeremy continued. "When Europeans first arrived in the New World, evidence suggests that, in addition to finding Native American encampments, they also found villages of Bigfoots."

Aisling Tolliver waved her hand in the air. "Excuse me, but shouldn't that be Bigfeet?" She looked hopefully at Miss March, who sometimes gave extra credit during reports, but the teacher appeared to be cleaning her glasses.

"Bigfoots," said Jeremy.

"Let's move along to the new evidence you mentioned," said Miss March.

Jeremy clicked to the next slide, a woodcut of a Pilgrim

village, where a man in kneesocks and knickers and a hat with a curled brim appeared to be trading a sack of marbles for a machete. The creature holding the machete was tall and bearded and broad-shouldered and, apparently, naked, except for a thick coat of fur.

"This woodcut," he said, "which I found after extensive research in the archives of the Standish Historical Society, is thought to depict a scene from the village that became our town, Standish. For all we know, we could be attending classes on the bones of the Bigfoots."

He paused, letting his words echo, which they did, until Austin armpit farted again. Olivia was braiding Sophie's hair, and in the front row Hayden Morganthal was resting his melon-shaped head on his forearms and snoring softly.

Jeremy swiped his sweaty palms against his pants. He hoped nobody would ask for details about the Standish Historical Society, which was just a collection of liquor-store cardboard boxes in Mrs. Bradon's garage. Mrs. Bradon lived downtown, and her great-grandfather Grayson Standish had been one of the town's fathers. She kept old maps and newspapers, handbills, and town tax returns piled in boxes in her garage, and let Jeremy look at them, after he promised not to make a mess.

Jeremy pushed on, clicking to slides that explained Bigfoot biology. "Once thought to be descended from the great apes of Africa, scientists now believe that Bigfoots are simply hominids who evolved at the same time as Neanderthal man, with certain musculoskeletal differences including extreme height and broad musculature that allowed them to become efficient hunter-gatherers in the Northeast and Pacific Northwest. Most Bigfoots are believed to be omnivores, eating flesh as well as flora. They are said to stand between seven and eight feet tall, weighing anywhere from three to five hundred pounds, and are covered with coarse, curling dark fur."

Another slide.

"Is that from *The National Enquirer*?" asked tattletale Meghan Carpenter, who sat next to Aisling in the back row.

"It's been widely reprinted," Jeremy said.

Miss March, who'd spent a lot of time instructing her class about what constituted reputable source material, made a mark in her notebook. Jeremy winced and went on.

"For hundreds of years, evidence suggests that Bigfoots and humans worked side by side to turn America from a nation of farms and homesteads to a land of towns, then cities. Bigfoots plowed the fields and cleared the forests." He showed a picture of what might have been two Bigfoots

41

or just two extremely large men in overalls and wide-brimmed hats standing next to a wagon full of lumber.

"Bigfoots helped build the railroads." Another slide, this one showing a crowd of men—one of whom towered head and shoulders above the others—posing proudly in front of a track.

"Evidence suggests that sometimes Bigfoots and humans would marry and have children."

"Eww!" squealed Lucy Jones.

Jeremy clicked to a sepia-toned family photograph, another discovery from the depths of the Bradon collection. The husband was an enormous, hulking man, tall and wide and heavily whiskered. His wife was clearly human, with a hint of amusement in the tilted corners of her mouth. The husband's free hand rested on the shoulder of a big, thick-necked boy who was staring at the ground so that most of his face was invisible to the camera. The wife was holding on to a freckle-faced girl with two long braided pigtails and the same smile as her mother.

"But as the march of progress continued, humans began to realize that their Bigfoot neighbors were different . . . and the Bigfoots began exploring means of controlling their fur and extreme size."

Jeremy clicked, then wiped his hands again and stole

a glance at the classroom. Hayden Morganthal was fast asleep. Sophie was now working on Olivia's hair. Aisling had a textbook open in her lap and was reading ahead in science.

Jeremy sighed. *Just wait,* he thought. *Wait until I find them. Wait until I show you they're real.*

The next slide showed a canvas-covered wagon with a poster on the side advertising "Snake Oil Scalp Tonic." Other posters offered love potions, slimming belts, various liniments, and lotions including—Jeremy zoomed in until the class could see it—Dr. McLaughlin's All-Natural Wildroot Hair Removing Crème. "Troubled by unwanted hair?" the text read. "Twice-a-day application of Dr. McLaughlin's All-Natural Wildroot Hair Removing Crème will eliminate unsightly whiskers from any portion of the anatomy, small or large, and permanently prevent their return!"

"Wasn't that just for, like, ladies' mustaches?" asked Austin the Armpit Farter. Austin had red hair and freckles and a smirky grin that allowed teachers to identify him as a troublemaker before he'd actually made any trouble.

"That's what they want you to believe," said Jeremy.

"Who's 'they'?" Austin inquired.

Jeremy clicked to the next slide, ignoring his classmate's questions. "Sadly, humans turned on their former friends and neighbors, labeling them freaks and abominations, forcing Bigfoots into hiding. The unfortunate Bigfoots who had the misfortune to be captured by hostile humans were displayed in circuses and traveling sideshows."

The worst slide, the one that always made him feel sick, came next. "BEHOLD LUCILLE, the FAMED and ORIGINAL BEARDED LADY!" blared a poster nailed to the wall above a cringing, fur-covered human-size creature in a cage. "IS SHE HUMAN? IS SHE BEAST? BORN with a FULL HEAD OF HAIR, her BEARD was APPARENT AT BIRTH and now she is COVERED WITH A PELT OF THICK FUR FROM HEAD TO TOE. Experts consider her ONE of the WONDERS OF THE MODERN AGE."

"My Nanna's got a mustache," volunteered Lucy Jones. "Maybe she's a Bigfoot!"

Jeremy, who thought Lucy had a bit of a mustache herself, hurried through the slides, eager to get away from the image of the furred but unmistakably female Bigfoot cowering behind the bars of her cage. If he found a Bigfoot, he'd make sure it was treated better than that—not locked up, not shown off for money. He'd be kind; he'd figure out its language (or teach it English) and make sure it had a comfortable place to live, with lots of space. He'd never keep a Bigfoot locked up . . . at least, he'd only lock one up until he figured out how to make it understand that he was its friend, not its enemy.

Jeremy showed his classmates pictures of footprints with rulers set beside them, proof that they hadn't been made by bears. He clicked through newspaper reports of campers who'd been awakened by strange noises and seen gigantic, hairy creatures running away—upright, on two legs—with their coolers and supplies. He lingered on a newspaper clipping with a picture of Milford Carruthers, a Standish resident, identified in the caption as "Famed Bigfoot Hunter," and his quote, which Jeremy knew by heart: "Given the preponderance of evidence, of sightings and reports down through the years, we must come to the obvious conclusion that Bigfoots are real, and that they live among us."

In the back row, Anthony Palmore, one of the smart kids who always turned in his homework on time, raised his hand. Anthony's button-down blue shirt was neatly ironed, his blue jeans had creases, and his sneakers were pristine. Anthony's mother, Jeremy thought, would never forget to take Anthony for his haircuts. Jeremy curled his toes inside his shoes. "Yes?"

"If they're real," said Anthony, "then why hasn't anyone found one? That picture you showed us was taken in the nineteen sixties, right?"

"Nineteen sixty-seven," said Jeremy, and jerked his neck to flip his long hair out of his eyes.

"And that's the most recent one?"

"They've gotten better at hiding," Jeremy said. "They've probably figured out how to grow their own food and tap into the power system without anyone knowing." He thought of the news reports of bears raiding a campsite in California two years ago. The campers had said they'd seen bears, but the footprints hadn't looked like bear prints, the police had said, but feet. *Big* feet. Jeremy was sure those weren't bears the campers had seen, but the investigators had never confirmed anything, and Jeremy knew his classmates would be brutal if he brought it up.

"While we're looking for them, I bet they're paying attention to us. They're probably online," he said instead.

"Try www.bigfoot.com," said Lucy Jones with a smirk.

"If they've gotten better at hiding, shouldn't we have gotten better at seeking?" asked Anthony. "Don't we have infrared sensors?"

"Bigfoots wouldn't show up on sensors any differently than humans," Jeremy said.

"What about drones or something?"

The back of Jeremy's neck prickled underneath his collar. He flicked his hair off his face again. "If you were a

Bigfoot," he said, keeping his voice level, "don't you think you'd be smart enough to figure out how to not be spotted by a drone?"

"The one in the picture doesn't look too smart," said Austin, hunching over, imitating the Bigfoot's pose and expression. Everyone laughed.

With his face burning, Jeremy dropped the remote on Miss March's desk—although "threw" might have been a more accurate word. "I'm done," he said, and stalked back to his seat. He knew how his afternoon would proceed: the call to the principal's office; the recess spent with the school counselor, Mrs. Dannicker, who had a sloping shelf of a bosom and whose sweaters were usually dotted with dabs of egg or tuna salad from her lunch. Mrs. Dannicker would ask him to discuss his interest in Bigfoots, and the difference between a "hobby" and an "obsession," and how was he getting along with his classmates, which would eventually lead to the question she always asked him, the one Jeremy thought was the only one she actually cared about: "How are things at home?"

At his desk Jeremy stared down at his textbooks and imagined how it must have been for the Bigfoots. One day they were living in villages and towns, friends and neighbors to the humans. Then the talk started.

They don't go to church, the ministers would say from their pulpits.

They don't come to school, the teachers would note.

They never wear shoes, the women would whisper. *Maybe, when they're alone, not even clothes!*

Why are they so big? Why are they so hairy?

They're not like us. Just like Jeremy wasn't like his exceptional brothers. He was lucky, he thought, that his parents still fed him and clothed him and let him live in their house, instead of displaying him in a cage and making people pay for a look.

Step right up to see the perfectly average boy, he thought, and scrubbed the heels of his hands against his stinging eyes as the bell rang. He heard his classmates gathering their books, chattering and laughing, and Lucy Jones saying, "I can't believe he did the exact same report again!"

When he looked up, the classroom lights had been turned back on, the room had emptied, and Miss March was sitting at the desk next to his. If she'd been angry (because he had, basically, repeated his project from the previous spring), if she'd been bored, if she'd threatened to flunk him, that all would have been fine. But Miss March looked concerned, the way his mother looked, on the rare occasions when she noticed him . . . like at Ben, when he'd gotten a concussion during the state semifinals, or at Noah, when *Nature* had asked him to rewrite his paper on stellar parallax before they'd publish it. Miss March's eyes were soft, and her voice was very gentle when she spoke.

"I apologize for your classmates," she said. "They should have listened to you with more respect."

Jeremy shrugged and started to gather his books. He didn't want sympathy, especially not from a teacher. Miss March put her hand on his arm. "I don't know if I've ever mentioned this in class, but I had a twin sister."

Jeremy swallowed a sigh and readied himself for Well-Meaning Grown-Up Speech #37: You're Special Too.

"She was different than I was," Miss March continued.

Of course she was, Jeremy thought. *Smarter. Faster. Stronger. Better.*

"She had multiple sclerosis—do you know what that is?"

Startled, Jeremy shook his head. This speech wasn't going where he'd imagined.

"It's a disease. People who have it sometimes can't walk or talk. They look different. My sister used a wheelchair, and she could communicate, but her speech wasn't clear. Most people didn't understand her." Miss March looked

away, toward the window. "Most people didn't try."

In the light from the windows, Jeremy saw that his teacher's white hair was fine, that her pink lipstick had worked its way into the tiny lines around her top lip.

"I know what it's like to feel like you're the child your parents forgot about. Between my sister's medical issues—the doctors and the therapy and all of it—it felt sometimes like I wasn't even there. Like I could be turning somersaults, or standing on my head in the middle of the kitchen, and my mom would say, 'Did Stephanie eat her lunch?' and my dad would say, 'I was on the phone with the insurance company about reimbursements.'" Miss March managed a smile. "But I worked hard to carve out my own niche—do you know what that means?—and I made some good friends." She patted Jeremy's arm. "It took time, but I found my way."

Jeremy wondered if Miss March had noticed that he had no friends among his classmates, that all the kids, even the troublemakers like Austin and the lazy lumps like Hayden Morganthal, thought he was a weirdo and a freak . . . and these were kids who'd known him his whole life. How would time help?

"You'll be fine," she said, and Jeremy nodded and zipped up his backpack and put it over his shoulders before he thought to ask, "What happened to your sister?"

Miss March had been straightening her stacks of paper. At Jeremy's question, she went very still. "She died," she said after a moment. "When we were—when she was sixteen."

Jeremy didn't know what to say to that. He'd hardly thought of teachers as having once been children, let alone children to whom terrible things happened. "Have a good weekend," he managed, and she gave him a sad smile, and then he was out the door, walking fast, with his head down and his thumbs hooked under his backpack straps.

The kids at school would never understand him, and it would probably take his parents a few weeks to notice if he ran away from home ("Honey, does it seem like there's more food left over from dinner?" he could hear his mother asking. "Should we call someone?" His dad would think for a minute, then shrug).

He would keep looking. He had one friend, one friend who believed him, and that was enough. He would continue his research and his explorations. He'd find a Bigfoot, and when he did, his parents, his classmates, his teachers, and the whole world would know his name.

CHAPTER 4

Alice

ALICE STEPPED OUT OF LEE'S CAR AND INTO the drowsy late-summer heat, thinking that her new school strongly resembled a dilapidated summer camp. The big, dark log-cabin lodge sat slumped on top of the hill. Lush vegetable gardens edged up against soccer fields with raggedy nets in the goals. Down a short slope was a lake with a half dozen banged-up canoes and battered kayaks pulled up onto the sandy shore, and a stack of sun-bleached, stained, and fraying life jackets were piled beside them. Alice remembered something from the school's welcoming letter, about how their "picturesque new lakeside campus" would "let our learners and guides live in harmony with nature, with the elements of earth and air and water, and the cycles of the moon." The school's founders emphasized that they tried to recycle or "freecycle" everything they needed, "sourcing" material from donations and barter. She wondered if any of the parents had gotten here, taken one look at how shabby everything was, and immediately asked for their money back.

The sound of drums echoed through the humid air. Across the soccer field, a tall, stick-skinny man was banging on a set of bongo drums, and a short, plump woman whose face was painted orange was doing a kind of twirling, skipping dance beside him.

"Welcome to Eden! The Land of Love!" the woman was singing. No one seemed to find this unusual. Parents greeted each other with smiles and hugs, kids exchanged grins and high fives. Alice sidled up to Lee, who gave her a sympathetic look, then began unloading her bags and carrying them to a tree where a sign reading "12-Year-Old Learners" had been taped to the trunk.

"Learners?" Alice said.

"We prefer that term." The short woman with the orange face paint had skipped up beside Alice. She had a wreath of flowers on her head and half-moon-shaped stains soaking her T-shirt underneath her armpits. "We believe in lifelong learning, and that all of us are students. Students in the school of life!"

Alice pressed her lips together so this woman, who was obviously an authority of some kind, wouldn't see her laugh. Did the School of Life hand out diplomas? Could you graduate with honors?

"Instead of students and teachers, we use the words 'learners' and 'guides,'" said the woman. "I'm Lori, by the way. Lori Moondaughter. My partner, Phil, and I are the founders of the Center."

Alice frowned. "The website said the Center was founded by Lori Weinreb."

The woman's smile wavered. "I changed it," she said. "I'm renouncing the patriarchal practice of daughters always taking their father's names." She stood on her tiptoes, bringing her painted face close to Alice's ear. "Also, I hated my old last name."

Lori captured both of Alice's hands in her own. She pressed them together and squeezed. "We are so glad you're here! We're so glad to be part of your village and so glad that you're going to be part of ours. With all our hearts"— Lori dropped Alice's hands and placed her right hand on her chest, atop the organ in question—"we welcome you."

"Thank you," Alice said. She made herself smile at Lori, then looked over at her luggage, wondering if she could quickly empty out the clothes and books and photographs she'd brought with her, then fold herself up inside the trunk and get Lee to smuggle her back to New York.

"Now," said Lori, "Miss Merriweather told me all about you. I'm afraid there aren't too many of you twelve-year-olds. Six boys and four girls, but just three of you now. In a few weeks you'll have a learner named Jessica Jarvis joining the village. Oh! Let me introduce you to Riya Amrit!"

Lori wrapped her arms around the shoulders of a slim, composed-looking girl with lush eyebrows and eyelashes and a graceful, contained way of moving. Her thick, dark hair was pulled back in a ponytail—a neat one, Alice noted, and her teeth were very even and white.

"Riya," Lori announced, "is one of the top-rated fencers in her age group." She smiled at Riya, who smiled back.

"I'm Alice," Alice said.

Riya nodded. "Welcome."

Lori latched on to another girl.

"Oh, and here's Taley. Taley Nudelman, Alice Mayfair."

"Hello," snuffled Taley, who was tall and pale with freckles and curly blond hair tucked under a bandanna.

She wore an orange jumper, with pockets made of blue fabric with white stars. There were pink high-top basketball sneakers on her feet, and she sounded so congested Alice was surprised she could say anything. "Weldcombe dto our learning commbunity."

"Can you two show Alice around?" Lori peered toward a pair of card tables whose metal legs appeared to be sinking into the lawn in front of the Lodge. One table held a trio of plastic bowls; the other a plastic platter of cut-up carrots and pita bread sliced into triangles. "I think we're running out of hummus." She hurried away.

Taley rolled her eyes. "I hopbe you like hummus," she said. "We eadt it, like, all the time."

"The hummus isn't so bad," said Riya. "The lentil loaf's the problem."

"Oh, Godtb, don'bt mention the lentil loaf," said Taley, and sneezed twice. "Allergies," she said, and waved her hand at the woods and the fields. "Mold, dirtb, pollens, dander . . ."

"If you're allergic to all of that, then how come you're going to school in the woods?" Alice asked.

"Her parents are friends with the Weinrebs," said Riya.

"Moondb Daughterbs," Taley said, and blew her nose.

Riya nodded. "Right. So Taley's parents sent her and

her brother and two sisters, so Phil and Lori would have some students."

"We were volunteerebd as tribudte. This will be my fourth yeardb atdb the Center. Lucky me." Taley sniffled, and Alice followed her two classmates to a small and slightly tilted cabin with two sets of bunk beds and cubbies built into the walls. Raw sap oozed down one of the boards in the corner, and the floors looked uneven.

Taley saw Alice staring. "Yeah, the campus usedb to dbe on an old farm upstate, but there were zoning issues."

"The neighbors complained about the compost heap," Riya said. "Runoff. And smell."

"So Lori and Phil found this spot. Itb was an oldb campgroundb." Taley set her backpack on the bottom bunk of one set of bunks, then looked at Alice. "You candb pick your bedb."

Alice claimed the second bottom bunk—big as she was, she could only imagine a top bunk sagging within inches of her bunkmate's face. "How about you?" she asked as Riya climbed on top of Taley's bunk. "How'd you end up here?"

"I fence," said Riya.

"That's, like, all she dboes," said Taley. "That and gymnastibs. Phil and Lori letd her do academics for an hour in the morningb, thenb she just works with her coach." She sniffled, blew her nose, and turned to Alice. "What's your thingb?"

Alice thought. "Does everyone here have a thing?"

"For the most part," Riya said. She was pulling books out of her backpack, *The Noble Art of the Sword* and *The Inner Game of Fencing* and *A Basic Foil Companion*. "Kelvin Atwater—you'll meet him later—he does magic. Not actual magic," she said, seeing Alice's face. "Magic tricks."

"Sleightb ofb handb," Taley confirmed, spreading a pink-and-purple comforter on her bed.

"What's your thing?" Alice asked Taley, who looked at her and frowned.

"I havbe allergies," she said.

"Oh," said Alice. She wondered if a thing could be a talent, or a problem, like Taley's allergies. Like her own hair. Like her own everything. Did "trying to disappear" count as a thing?

"And she's extremely creative," Riya said. Taley gave her a look that was equal parts affection and exasperation. "She can sew," said Riya in the same tone she'd use to announce that Taley could fly, and pointed toward an old-fashioned sewing machine and a bag of fabric in the corner.

Alice was quiet, hoping they would drop the topic of her own special thing. She made her bed with the fancy cotton sheets Felicia had packed, slipping her down pillows into their crisp cases, and set up her toothpaste, toothbrush, and family-size bottles of extra-strength conditioner in the bathroom.

Taley was there putting away a small ceramic pitcher that she said was called a neti pot. "Don'bt ever dringk outb ob itb," she said, then considered. "Probably don'bt eben touch itd." She filled the pot with warm water, leaned over the sink, tilted her head, and stuck the spout into her left nostril. "It's for congestiondb," she said as Alice backed out of the bathroom.

Someone had slipped a daily schedule under the door. Alice picked up the piece of paper and started to read out loud. "Each morning begins with a choice of Morning Meditation, Sun Salutations, or Intentional Weeding.'"

"It's regular weeding," said Riya, who must have noticed Alice's confusion. "You just have to look like you're thinking about it." She unzipped a duffel bag and pulled out a sword. *A foil*, Alice thought. She looked out the window and saw a few grown-ups—learning guides, she reminded herself—walking past. One of the men was wearing a floaty white skirt, and one of the women had a bright red buzz cut and a ring through her septum.

"Like, you pull out a weed and look at it for a minute, like you're sorry you disrupted its experience," said Riya. "Just be glad they got rid of Contemplative Canoeing."

"Why?" Alice asked. She was beginning to get the idea that at the Experimental Center, there was a story behind everything.

"Last year Jared Cagan fell asleep in a canoe and floated, like, five miles downriver. Lori and Phil had to go into town and borrow a motorboat from one of the guys at the gas station . . . and you can probably guess how Lori and Phil feel about burning fossil fuels," Riya said.

"Alsobd, the townies thoughtdb we were freaks," Taley called from the bathroom.

Alice nodded, then wandered toward the door, managing to bump into another sword that was resting against the wall.

"Careful!" Riya snapped, as the sword clattered to the floor. Nimbly, Riya hopped off the top bunk. Alice mumbled an apology—the first of many she'd be making, she thought—and finally walked outside.

Except for the gloomy wooden lodge, the Center looked like it had been slapped together over a weekend, by people who had one saw, one hammer, and absolutely no experience. The half dozen cabins for the learners, the coops for the chickens, and the goat pen all looked like they'd fall over if the wind blew too hard. She walked past the animals—a flock of clucking chickens, a few grumpy-looking goats—and toward the forest, where she spotted a dirt path that seemed to lead through the trees.

Alice began to walk along the packed dirt, her sneakers scuffling through brown pine needles. The leaves overhead were so dense that the sunshine was faint and tinted greenish gold. She could hear a frog croak, a bird chirp, a small something scampering away as she approached, first walking, then running. Faster and faster she went through the golden-green, swinging her arms, lifting her legs higher, scooting over roots, leaping over fallen branches. She'd never been in a situation or a place like this, alone in a forest, where she didn't have to wait up for her classmates or follow her teacher, where she could go where she wanted, as fast as she could. Her heart pumped hard; her soles slapped the dirt. Her hair burst out of its elastics and her braids unraveled until the Mane was flying out behind her. Alice pumped her arms and kicked her legs out hard, hearing the rhythm of her feet and her breath, her ears full of the thunder of her own heartbeat; feeling her blood-flushed face, the sweat streaming down her cheeks and arms and back; smelling leaves and grass and growing things, the mineral tang of lake water, and faint notes of the approaching autumn.

She ran and ran, loving the sensation of her body at work, relishing the quiet and the solitude, pushing herself to go faster and faster until the path ended at the shore of the lake—Lake Standish, she reminded herself. Standish was the name of the lake and the name of the town and, she bet, the name of the town's main street or high school or both. Breathing hard, Alice cupped her hands in the water and rinsed her face, then let a palmful of water trickle from her crown down through her hair. Her shirt was plastered to her body, her shoes were filthy, her hair was already matted with branches and leaves, but she couldn't remember a time when she'd felt so wonderful.

Sitting by the water to catch her breath, she closed her eyes and listened. Little wavelets lapped gently at the toes of her shoes. She could hear the trill of a bird, the burst and flutter of wings . . . and, very faintly, voices.

Alice stood up, squinting across the lake. She didn't see anything but more trees . . . but she was sure she'd heard something, a girl's voice, singing. She sat down again, slipping off her shoes and planting her feet in the water, eyes shut, listening, feeling the Mane hanging warm and heavy against her back, thinking that maybe this place would be all right, if she could run like this every day, away from the school and the students (the Center and the learners, she reminded herself), away from everything, even her own thoughts.

When Alice trotted back to the Center, she found tall, skinny, face-painted Phil standing in the middle of the soccer field, pounding a cowbell with a stick. "Village assembly!" he called in a high, thin voice. His beard waggled in time to the stick strikes. "Everyone meet at Mother Tree!"

Alice joined the crowd of kids moving toward the big tree Phil was pointing at. They were, she thought, a motley crew. Some of the girls had put on makeup and colorful woven bracelets and had painted their nails and dressed in outfits that looked both clean and planned; others, like Riya, just wore shorts and T-shirts and seemed unconcerned if their ponytails were crooked or their fingernails were bare. Taley was still in her orange, blue, and white jumper and pink sneakers, but she'd discarded her bandanna and tied hanks of purple yarn at the ends of the ponytails she'd fashioned. A few of the boys wore the cool-kid uniform of droopy, oversize basketball shorts, enormous sneakers, and baseball caps turned backward that Alice had seen in New York City. But she also saw one boy dressed all in black—black pants, black shoes, black long-sleeved shirt—with his hair dyed black and styled in a Mohawk. A girl wore head-to-toe tie-dye, and another girl was all in white, with hair that hung past her waist and a skirt so long that its hem dragged on the grass . . . and nobody stared. There were *Doctor Who* T-shirts and acid-washed jeans, fringed boots and leather sandals, fingernails in shades from pearly white to inky black (both boys and girls had painted nails), pierced noses and pierced eyebrows, and no one was making a big deal about anyone else.

Alice followed the pack to Mother Tree and took a seat in the grass.

Everyone here has a thing, she thought, remembering what Taley had said. Looking at her new classmates, she wondered if it was true . . . and, if it was, what her thing might be.

"Welcome, all," said Lori. She lifted her arms, palms up, and closed her eyes, and stood silently for a very long time. Just when Alice was beginning to wonder if she'd fallen into a trance, or maybe just asleep, she began in a slow, almost eerie voice: "The light within me salutes and honors the light within you."

Alice had been around Felicia's yoga instructor long enough to mutter, "Namaste."

Taley Nudelman pulled a pile of yarn and a needlepoint pillowcase out of her backpack. She sneezed, then sighed, reaching for one of the half dozen undyed cotton handkerchiefs she carried instead of paper tissue ("They're vbery bidg on reuse," she whispered when she saw Alice staring).

"We are all, every one of us, creators of the light. Let's take a moment to honor that sacred specialness," said Lori.

Riya hunched over a fencing book, making crisp swishing motions with an index finger. Two rows ahead, a boy of eight or nine who seemed to have twice the normal allotment of teeth flicked a paper football at the back of another boy's head, and a few kids down, the tie-dye girl was drumming a complicated rhythm on her thighs.

Here we go, thought Alice as Lori continued. "Let us seek to love, not to hate. Let us seek to heal, not hurt. Let the future stand revealed. Let love prevail."

"Let Kate have lost her recipe for tandoori tofu," a boy behind Alice whispered as Lori, face flushed and arms stretched up to the sky, concluded, "May the wind be always at your back, may a friend be always at your side, and may the Rainbow always touch your shoulder."

Lori sat down, fluffing her curly hair with her fingers,

and Phil, who had a guitar slung around his neck, got to his feet. He was so tall and thin, and Lori was so short and round. Alice thought that, together, they looked like an exclamation point and a period. She considered whispering this observation to one of her bunkmates, but Taley was doing something with her wool, and Riya was still concentrating on her book and whatever fencing match was happening in her head.

"And now," said Phil, "a few words about words. You'll notice that we've done away with the titles of 'student' and 'teacher.' Because, the truth is, we're all part of a village, a community where everyone's an educator and everyone's a learner. Calling you 'students' puts us"—he raised one hand high in the air—"above you." He lowered his other hand toward the ground. "When really"—he floated his hands toward one another until they met at the end of his beard—"we are all the same. And along those lines . . ."

Alice half listened as Phil talked about how insults, obviously, were not allowed at the Center. Neither was "body talk"—either positive or negative. "Telling someone they look nice centers the conversation on their physical selves where what we want is to be mindful of our souls," he said. A few of the older kids snickered.

"Couldb dbe worse," Taley whispered. "Last year, we

godt a three-hourdb lecture on Your Carbon Foobtprint."

"And now," said Phil, "let's meet our learning guides."

The people formerly known as teachers, Alice thought, as Phil introduced a woman with pale, freckled skin and dreadlocks.

"Kara comes to us from the Kripalu Center, where she trained as a monk for three years."

Kara folded her hands in prayer against her chest and wished them *namaste.* An amiable, round-faced guy named Clem was in charge of the gardens; a serious-looking woman with a cap of steel-gray curls named Abigail would be "your guide through the wonders of poetry and Shakespeare." Their math guide was a stocky person with a neat goatee and a skirt named Terry.

"Terry's preferred pronouns are ze, hir, and hirs," Phil said. "And Kate's in charge of the kitchens and all things culinary."

A very large woman with a crown of dark-brown braids stepped forward. She was possibly the largest person Alice had ever seen who wasn't on one of the extreme weight-loss TV shows that Felicia liked—the ones where they'd sometimes have to cut a hole in a wall to get a person out of a house so that he or she could begin their fitness journey, a trip that typically involved gym equipment donated by the same companies that advertised during the show, and an attractive trainer who yelled a lot. The large woman gave an abrupt nod, then stepped back again, staring at her heavy leather boots.

"Looks like Kate enjoys her work," whispered a boy a few rows back, and a girl giggled. "Would you even want a skinny cook?"

Alice tried not to sigh as she wrapped her arms around herself and hunched her head down, trying to look smaller. As the introductions continued, Alice looked down at the lake, then over toward the forest. She'd gone through this process so many times, at so many different kinds of schools, but it never got easy. New kids to meet, new routines to learn, a new campus to get to know, and then holding her breath, waiting for the inevitable moment when the other kids would turn on her.

Alice pictured her bed, with its soft down pillows, white down comforter, and crisp white sheets. She thought about how at night, instead of smog and city lights, she would be able to see the stars. Maybe she would sleep deeply, with no bad dreams, and wake up to see the sunrise over the lake. Maybe she'd get up early and she'd run in the forest, feeling the dew soak her sneakers and the cool air against her face, her feet skimming the paths, jumping over fallen trees and snarls of branches and brambles, leaping lightly over streams, running and running until her lungs burned in her chest and the world swam in starbursts in front of her eyes and her muscles felt warm and easy against her bones, like she could sit still and listen all day.

Eventually, she knew, things would go wrong, because things always did, no matter how careful she was, no matter how hard she tried. At some point in October or November, Alice would expose herself as different, abnormal, like at the École, when she'd bent over in gym class and split her pants right down the middle, or at Swifton, where, on parents' day, one of the mothers, glimpsing Alice from behind with the Mane tucked under her hood, had thought that Alice was a boy and had yelled at her for being in the girls' room.

No matter how it happened, she would do something or say something or trip or rip or break something and give herself away. That was the way it always was. But until that day came, she would enjoy this place, with its quiet woods and its oddball "learning guides" and the kids, some of whom seemed to be almost as weird as she was.

CHAPTER 5

Millie

THE MORNING AFTER THE ELDERS' MEETING, the other littlies—Jacobus and Tulip, six-year-old Madder, and four-year-old Florrie, who was already bigger than Millie—filed into the underground school-burrow.

Millie had been excused for the morning. After First Breakfast she had nodded solemnly at her father, given her anxious mother a smile, then clambered up the Lookout Tree. From her perch she would watch the new school across the lake and do her lessons by herself, and at the snackle, which was served between Second Breakfast and lunch, she'd report to Old Aunt Yetta and her father about what she'd seen. She was to count how many No-Furs there were, how many grown-ups and how many littlies, how many vehicles they had, whether she saw any weapons, and most important, whether the setup on the lakeshore seemed to be permanent or temporary. Old Aunt Yetta had lent her the Tribe's single pair of antique binoculars, and Maximus had given her a new notebook and a black felt-tipped pen. So far Millie had written her name on the cover with a flourish and made note of the eight cars that had come down the dirt path, as well as the sixteen littlies who'd gotten out. She was looping the binoculars' leather carrying case around her neck and readjusting her position when a furry head popped out of the school-burrow door and a voice announced, "Teacher Greenleaf says it's time for you to come down."

Millie sighed. There were only three other littlie girls in the Yare Tribe. Florrie was such a baby that she nibbled on her cheek-fur when no one was looking, and Madder was almost an Elder. Tulip was the only girl close to Millie's age. Tulip was tall and strong and sure-footed. Tulip was always quiet, always good. Last Halloween she'd decided to stay home, virtuously announcing that safety was more important to her than candy.

Millie and Tulip did not get along.

"I am occupied," said Millie.

"Teacher says now," Tulip said.

"Nugget," sighed Millie—a Yare expression of regret—and started to scramble down the tree. Tulip's schoolbooks were arranged in a neat stack beneath her arm, and her light-brown fur, neatly brushed and dressed with a dark-blue bow, was already beginning to darken at the tips of her ears.

More unfairness, Millie thought. When Millie was born, her birth-fur, called duff, was pure white. No one in the Tribe, not even Old Aunt Yetta, had ever seen a newborn with white duff, and none of them knew what it meant—only that it had never happened before. Her parents tried to assure each other that this was probably normal, and that they'd each had or heard of relatives whose light fur had darkened over time. But Millie's fur never became a normal Yare shade, brown or chestnut or reddish or black. Instead it stayed silvery gray and was not coarse or curly, but as light and sleek as corn silk.

Nor did Millie's oddness stop with her strange fur. Most of the Yare were tall and solid. Millie was short and small. With her thin wrists and delicate fingers, she was the littlest Yare anyone had ever seen. Although Millie had spoken early, she'd been slow to walk, slow to run, and she'd never been able to to keep up with her packmates. Worse than all that, though, was the way she pestered her folks about the No-Fur world and why the Yare lived the way they did, questioning every rule and restriction that other littlies simply accepted.

"Why are we having to be quiet?" she had asked when she was three years old and Teacher Greenleaf had shushed her six times before morning snackle.

"Because the No-Furs will hear us," Teacher Greenleaf lectured, "and then do us harm."

"Why can't I go with you?" she asked Maximus each month, when her father put on his biggest hat and longest coat and put an empty packsack over his back. He was preparing for the Mailing, a dangerous mission entrusted to the Leader of the Tribe. The Yare supported themselves, living off the land, sewing their own clothes, eating the food they'd grown or made . . . but for as long as Millie had been alive, the Yare had earned No-Fur currency by selling things they made in an Etsy shop called Into the Woods. Millie wasn't sure whether Etsy was a person or a place, but she knew how it worked. Each month the members of the Tribe would give Maximus what they'd made: mittens and caps in bright colors; soft scarves and shrugs and woolen wraps; carved cutting boards and birdhouses; special scrubs and decoctions made with the herbs and leaves and blossoms the Yare would grow and gather—all labeled "Organic" and "Handmade." They'd wrap and package the goods for mailing, and then carefully glue on the No-Fur addresses that Old Aunt Yetta had printed, weigh each parcel, and cover it with the correct number of stamps.

Millie loved the night before the Mailing. At three, she'd declared herself the Package Inspector and would carefully examine each labeled parcel, tasting the No-Fur names and addresses on her tongue, imagining the different towns and states where the Yare-made goods would go. The next morning Maximus would gather up the goods and walk ten miles to the town of Standish. He'd drop the packages at the posting-office counter, all stamped and ready to go, and he'd use his key to open up the mailbox and take out whatever goods the Yare had ordered on-the-line—white sugar, and reading glasses, and the Snickers bars that all Yare loved.

When Millie was four, she'd tried to follow her father on the Mailing. He'd caught her, of course, and she'd been punished most severely: sent to her room every day after lessons were through, and then again after dinner. Worse than the punishment, worse than her father's anger, was the way her mother had cried until the fur on her face was sodden, holding Millie in a panicky grip and saying, over and over, that she didn't know what she'd do if she ever lost her Little Bit.

That should have been enough to end Millie's fascination with the No-Fur world, but it wasn't. Every night Millie would listen for voices coming from across the lake, the five miles of water that separated the Yare village from the campground where the No-Furs would come to pitch their tents and light their fires, roast their delicious-smelling meat on sticks, and sometimes, sing.

Tulip, of course, had no interest in No-Fur foods and No-Fur songs. Tulip was a head taller and much heavier than Millie, and she would probably rusticate first. As soon as her ear tips and the circles around her eyes were completely dark, she'd be an Elder, able to hold the Speaking Stick, a grown-up with a voice and with power. Tulip's parents, Millie knew, thought their daughter would be a much better Ruler than Millie, even though they'd never dared to say so to Maximus.

"Mill-ee." Tulip was tapping one large bare foot against the dirt. "I am losing the patience with you."

"Wait." Millie's sharp ears had picked up more car sounds. She scrambled back up the tree.

Across the water, a procession of cars was rolling down the dirt road, stirring up a cloud of dust. She could hear raised voices, slammed doors, the sound of drums and someone strumming a guitar, and No-Furs calling greetings, asking, "How was your summer?" and saying, "Good to see you!"

Millie was so excited that she could barely breathe. She wanted to jump up and down, to wave her arms and shout, "I'm here!" or go racing across the water. Instead, to calm herself, she sang a lullaby that Old Aunt Yetta had taught her.

"The summer wind, came blowin' in from across the sea," Millie sang softly. She watched a boy open the back end of a car and lift out a heavy bag and a suitcase. "It lingered there to touch your hair and walk with me," she sang. If she ever had the chance to audition for *The Next Stage*, she'd sing that song. She could see herself, in a silvery dress the exact color of her silvery fur, clutching the slim stalk of the microphone and closing her eyes as she sang. Except, in the daydream, she didn't have fur but skin, smooth, lovely skin, sometimes pinky white, sometimes golden brown, sometimes a radiant black that was almost blue. Human skin.

She closed her eyes and listened. There were women singing on the other side of the shore, their voices, thin and warbling, raised in a wobbly three-part harmony. *"When John Henry was a little baby, sittin' on his mama's knee . . ."*

By their third time through, Millie had the words and

the melody, and she joined in, perfectly in tune, when they began the song again. *"Picked up a hammer in his little right hand / said, 'Hammer gonna be the death of me, Lord, Lord / Hammer gonna be the death of me.'"* Only why would baby's own hammer be the death of him? Was there some hammer-related mishap in an upcoming verse?

Tulip was glaring at her. "If you don't stop with that racket, Teacher Greenleaf will be the death of you."

Millie ignored her. *I wish,* she thought as she stared across the lake, as if wishing could magically transport her over the miles, over the water, to the place where she wanted to be.

I wish there weren't Yare around all the time. The Elders loved her, she knew, but their love could feel like suffocation, like being crammed into an itchy sweater that had been too small for years.

I wish there weren't so many rules: "Millie, keep your voice down!" "Millie, try to keep up with your packmates!" "Millie, pay the attention!" "Millie, sit up with a straightness!"

I wish I was having the choice, she thought.

I wish I could leave here.

I wish I could sing.

CHAPTER 6

Alice

"GOOD MORNINGS, LEARNERS," SANG PHIL, FOUR weeks after Alice's arrival, as he stood outside of Bunk Ladybug's window. (The seventh-grade girls' bunk had been called Bunk Seven until the week before, when Phil and Lori decided that numbers were hierarchical and that hierarchies were, by their very nature, unfair, and had renamed all the bunks after insects and birds.) "The earth says hello!"

Alice peeked out the window to see that Phil had covered his narrow, rectangular face in face paint—lately he'd been favoring blue—and braided his beard. It hung like a second tongue, dangling at the center of his chest.

In the bed beside hers, Alice heard Taley sniffle, then reach for her inhaler, then her embroidery hoop, and the sound of Riya's steps as she danced through a fencing warm-up, slashing and stabbing at an imaginary opponent.

Alice had already been awake for an hour. She'd gone for her morning run through the woods and then walked back along the lakeshore to her cabin, with wet leaves slipping underneath her feet and a cool breeze ruffling her hair.

She got out of bed, cinched the elastic band around the Mane, made sure her socks weren't muddy, and pulled a fleece sweatshirt over her plain blue T-shirt, feeling grateful, the way she felt every time she changed her clothes, that the Center had no uniforms. Alice, and the rest of the student body, had been encouraged to treat fashion as "a vehicle for self-expression," which meant that you could wear anything, as long as it wasn't see-through or low-cut and it didn't have a logo or brand name ("Our bodies are not billboards for corporate America," Lori liked to say).

As the summer weather cooled and the air got crisp, with a wintry bite to the wind, Alice wore mostly yoga pants and fleece, elastic-waisted and oversize, clothes she hoped she wouldn't grow out of before the semester ended. Taley layered tights and leggings and long-sleeved thermal shirts beneath her hand-sewn jumpers, which she'd made with extra pockets for handkerchiefs and medication. Riya wore athletic gear, leggings made of sweat-wicking fabric, and a zippered nylon jacket that proclaimed her a member of the Junior National Fencing Team.

As Phil started up with his cowbell, the girls gathered their books and laptops and headed out of the cabin. Alice began her day with Intentional Weeding, while Taley did Morning Meditation. ("Butd really," she said, "I mostly justb sitb there andb sleeb.") Riya had gotten special permission to fence.

The next activity was Daily Conversation. With the learners assembled in a semicircle beneath Mother Tree, Phil and Lori would talk about the day, whether there was anything special planned (there usually wasn't), and whether there were any changes to the rules (there always were). Then the learners and guides would march to the Lodge for breakfast, the object of which, Alice sometimes thought, was for Kate, the Center's cook, to get as many grains as possible into otherwise normal food. There'd be seven-grain porridge and twelve-grain toast, and apples, which the Center got by the bushel from a neighboring orchard.

Learning sessions—which, in Alice's previous schools, had been called "classes"—were held outside during good weather. Abigail would take a group of kids down to the shores of the lake, and the learners would take turns reading aloud from and then discussing *Of Mice and Men*, or Terry would teach algebra underneath Mother Tree. There was another break before lunchtime. Alice would usually wander in the forest or take out a canoe with Taley. Riya would sometimes join them, resting on her belly in the middle of the boat with a book propped up in front of her.

Taley and Riya weren't her friends—they hardly even tried to talk to her, on the water or at Nutrition, when they all sat together at one of the two long tables that ran the length of the Lodge—but at least they weren't mean. Riya would press her lips together into a tight line and sigh when Alice knocked over the swords Riya had left by the door, or interrupted her practice, and Taley had snapped, "Didn'tb I tell you notb to touch itb?" after Alice had somehow elbowed Taley's neti pot to the floor, but they didn't go out of their way to torment her, which made them a nice change from her previous classmates.

Lunch, "Midmorning Nutrition," was at one o'clock. The food was, as Alice had feared, mostly vegetarian, with the occasional fish on Fridays (whatever enjoyment the learners might have found from the pan-fried flounder or grilled brook trout was severely diminished by Lori's lengthy predinner blessing, during which she'd urge everyone to "honor the soul and the spirit of this animal, that its flesh might enrich and strengthen us"). In the afternoons there were Specials—sports or music lessons, drama or choir. Alice worked in the garden alongside Clem, who had a cheerful round face and had spent six years following a band called Phish around before settling down at the Center. Then there was more free time, for homework or "quiet contemplation," which for the younger kids meant naps, and then dinner. Even though she missed cheeseburgers and steak, Alice was learning to like the food at the Center: lentil soups and black-bean burritos, vegetarian lasagna made with soy cheese, five-bean salad and curried tofu mash. Everything was made with fresh herbs and unusual spices; everything tasted interesting, which was an improvement over the meals at Swifton or Miss Pratt's.

Kate had noticed Alice on the third night, when Alice had asked for a second helping of lentil soup. "It's delicious," she said, and Kate, who wore black dresses and enormous white aprons and seemed to frown all the time, had given Alice a hard look.

"Cumin," she finally said.

A few nights later, when Alice complimented her on the whole-grain biscuits, Kate said, "Thank you." *If this keeps going,* Alice thought, *she'll say an entire sentence by Christmas . . .* but it ended up not taking that long. One night, after Alice had devoured the tofu tikka masala, Kate said, "I do cooking class Wednesday nights. If you're interested."

Alice was absolutely interested. When she arrived at the Lodge on Wednesday, Kate was waiting, with her hair covered in a kerchief, her body covered by a crisp white apron that hung past her knees. Alice looked around, but she didn't see any other learners. This was fine with her.

"Brioche," Kate announced, pulling out a basket of eggs, a crock of butter, and—after a quick glance over her shoulder—white sugar and white flour, which she removed from a locked cupboard at the back of the kitchen. "Cooking is a science," Kate began. She had a low, gruff voice, and she spoke so quietly that Alice had to lean close to listen. "Mostly, if you follow the recipe, you get what you wanted. Not like life," she said, and sighed. Before Alice could figure out how to ask Kate what that meant, Kate was sliding a thick cookbook across the table. *How to Cook Everything* was written on the cover. The book bristled with Post-it notes and scraps of paper. The pages were wavy, as if the book had gotten wet at some point. Some pages were spotted with gravy or grease or red wine, and almost every recipe had notes—ingredients crossed out, new ones added, asterisks indicating the dates they'd been cooked and if the kids had liked whatever it was.

By the end of her first month at the Center, Alice had cooked brioche and angel food cake and pound cake and was moving on to breads and soups. "Not bad," Kate would say, tasting a spoonful or a bite of whatever Alice had prepared, adjusting the seasoning, sometimes giving Alice one of her rare smiles. When the lesson was over, she'd let Alice wrap up a few cookies or slices of cake to take back to the bunk or to tuck into her backpack and eat after her run in the morning.

Alice was almost afraid to admit it, even to herself, but she liked the Experimental Center. Taley and Riya left her alone after she'd declined their invitations to learn how to fence or to sew, invitations they'd probably only offered to be polite. After Alice had turned them each down twice, it seemed like they'd made some secret agreement to keep their distance, which was fine with Alice. The three of them were unfailingly polite to one another. Riya and Taley would deal with whatever new havoc Alice had caused with a minimum of sighs and eye rolls.

Riya had a best friend, an older girl and fellow fencer named Alana, and everyone liked Taley, who could mend rips and tears and replace lost buttons.

Most of the guides were nice. Clem showed her how to make a salt scrub using coconut oil and the lavender the previous year's learners had grown and dried, and Terry, who taught math, turned out to be very patient, even when Alice needed things explained more than once.

Alice had her books of Greek mythology and her sketch pads, on which she drew pictures of flowers and the lake with the mountains rising behind it. She had the solitude of her morning runs and the pleasure of the little treats she'd tuck away. She was too busy to ever feel really lonely, or to feel bad when other kids got care packages or letters from home. The only mail she ever got were New York City–themed postcards from Lee and a note from Miss Merriweather that came on monogrammed stationery and said, *I hope you're doing well!*

Alice was feeling good that morning as she walked toward Daily Conversation, munching on a slice of banana-walnut bread, her body warm and relaxed after her run. She was so lost in her thoughts about the day ahead—English, then a walk in the woods, a nap after lunch, and then a cooking lesson—that she almost didn't notice the black Town Car cruising down the dirt path in a cloud of dust.

"Hey, watch outb!" Taley cried. Riya looked up from her book as the car jerked to a stop six inches from her hip.

A blank-faced chauffeur in a suit and black cap got out of the car, walked to the rear door, and pulled it open, and a girl who was about their age but who looked nothing like any of them, or like any other girl at the Center, emerged.

Her scent was what Alice noticed first, a sweet mixture of honeysuckle, raspberry, and coconut shampoo that gave her the smell of a fruit salad left out of the refrigerator for too long. The girl at the center of this aromatic cloud had shiny brown hair that hung in waves to the small of her back and a heart-shaped face with glossed, pouting lips. She wore a short black skirt, cinched tight at the waist, pointy-toed black patent-leather shoes, and a white silk blouse. Earrings twinkled from her lobes, and a gold bangle encircled her wrist. Her eyes were hidden behind dark glasses, but her frown wasn't hidden at all.

"What a dump," she said, and tilted her nose a few degrees higher into the air. "This is even worse than that farm we were at last year."

"Hey, your drivber almost hitb us," Taley said.

The girl tossed her hair. "You were standing in the middle of the road." She toed the dirt disdainfully. "Such as it is." Pulling off her dark glasses, she turned toward Alice. "And you are . . . ?"

Alice cleared her throat. "Alice Mayfair."

"She's frombd dNew York," said Taley.

"Congratulations." The girl didn't even try to sound sincere.

"You should be more careful," said Alice, feeling suddenly protective toward her cabin mates. Riya, who read fencing books while she walked between sessions, would probably wander right into traffic if there'd been any traffic at the Center for her to wander into, and Taley was so congested all the time that she probably couldn't hear cars approaching.

"Oh, really?" sneered the girl. Then she whirled, her skirt flaring, at the sound of Phil and Lori approaching, and put on the fakest smile Alice had ever seen. "Hello, guides!" she caroled. "I'm sorry I'm so late, but I'm finally here!"

CHAPTER 7

Jeremy

FOR YEARS JEREMY'S PARENTS, MARTIN AND Suzanne, clung to the idea that their youngest son was a musical prodigy. It had started when, in kindergarten, the music teacher had scribbled "shows promise!" beneath Jeremy's "Satisfactory" grade in chorus. Martin and Suzanne had seized on those two words with panicked desperation.

"Music," said Martin.

"Of course!" said Suzanne, and sighed deeply in relief.

They'd ushered little Jeremy into the dining room, a room they hardly ever used unless there were important matters to discuss or big decisions to be made. This was the room where Noah eventually decided between MIT and Caltech, the room where Ben would sit and meet with the college coaches who'd come calling.

"You are a musical prodigy!" his mother announced. "A genius," she added, after Jeremy just stared.

Jeremy might have just been a little kid, but he knew two things. The first was that, to keep his parents happy, he needed to be a standout in something. The second was that he was pretty sure he wasn't a musical prodigy; he was just okay at music, not great. But his parents were gazing at him with such love and such hope—the way he was used to seeing them look at his brothers—that Jeremy wanted to be that star they'd hoped for, a boy that they could love.

The oboe had been his father's suggestion. Jeremy had requested guitar lessons, but his parents told him that the oboe was more unusual and that Jeremy's mastery of a difficult instrument would give him more opportunities at youth orchestras and local symphonies and, eventually, at colleges.

"If there are six violinists and only one oboist, you're a shoo-in," his father explained.

"But what if I'm the best violinist?" Jeremy asked. He didn't want to play the violin—he wanted to play the guitar—but even a violin had to be better than an oboe.

89

Martin had frowned. "Oboist? Oboe player? Hon, do you know what it is?"

His parents went off to consult a dictionary. Jeremy noticed that his father hadn't even considered the possibility that Jeremy might be the best at something. Maybe they believed he was a prodigy, but it also seemed like they were, as his papa Frank liked to say, "hedging their bets" ("That's like when you pray for rain but dig a well while you're praying," Papa Frank had explained).

It was months before Jeremy learned to blow into the oboe's reed and produce a tone that sounded like music and not like a small animal moaning out its death throes. He'd practiced for an hour a day, grimly mastering scales and simple tunes, Purcell's "Air" and "Somewhere over the Rainbow." He tried not to be hurt when Shayna, the family's sheltie, crawled underneath his bed when he practiced, and he ignored his brothers when they covered their ears and offered him money and comic books in exchange for quiet.

"Very good," his teacher would tell him. Mr. McCrae, who played seven instruments, including the bagpipes, would praise Jeremy's diligence and hard work. "Nice effort," he'd say. "Keep it up!" Jeremy knew that wasn't the same as saying he'd played well, or that what he was playing was beautiful.

For a few years Jeremy's efforts with the oboe seemed to be enough to keep his parents happy. "And Jeremy's our musician," his mother would say after she got through describing Ben's latest feats on the football field or how Noah was planning on spending the summer working on some arcane proof with a mathematics professor from Princeton.

Jeremy played with the local youth orchestra and spent his summers in music camps. Finally, when he turned ten, his parents made some calls and got Jeremy a chance to apply for the Pre-College Division program at the prestigious Juilliard School in New York City. Jeremy was instructed to prepare two pieces of music for the panel, and so, in between rounds of Mario Kart and reading Steven Universe comics, he'd practiced "Hedwig's Theme" from the Harry Potter movies and "Sweet Child o' Mine" by Guns N' Roses, which he'd arranged himself.

His parents were practically glowing as they loaded up the car for the two-hour trip to the city. While Jeremy's father parked the car, Suzanne whisked Jeremy to a door where someone had Scotch-taped a sign that read "Auditions." Past the door was an auditorium, with rows of empty seats in front of a brilliantly lit stage. Up front, in the very first row, were an older man in a tweedy suit, a younger woman in a floor-sweeping dress with a color-ful embroidered top, and another woman, middle-aged, wearing jeans and a plaid shirt, hunched over a yellow legal pad.

"Jeremy," called the tweedy man in a rich, rolling voice. "If you would."

With sweat-slicked hands, Jeremy unfolded his sheet music and forced his wooden legs to deliver him to the stage. Even before he set his lips on the reed, even before he'd blown the first note, he knew there was no way that Juilliard would take him. He couldn't do anything new or special . . . and he could tell, in just ten minutes of being at Juilliard, that it was a place for rare and special people. His parents, his brothers, they belonged in places like this. Jeremy should be here only to deliver someone's lunch or take out their trash.

He finished "Sweet Child o' Mine" with a little swag-ger, knowing he had nothing left to lose. The tweedy man gave him a curt nod, and the woman in jeans looked over his head, toward the door.

"How'd it go?" asked Jeremy's father, who was waiting outside, keeping an eye on the car, which he'd had to park illegally.

"Fine!" said Suzanne in a voice that was too high

and too bright. Jeremy felt the air shift as his parents exchanged a glance. They'd never say anything out loud, and they'd try to treat him the same, but he knew that something had changed, permanently and profoundly. He had disappointed them . . . and he didn't know how to fix it, unless it turned out that there was something he was great at, and he was almost positive that there wasn't.

Back home, he'd put his oboe, in its hard plastic case, on a high shelf in his closet. Then he'd gone for a walk in the woods. Head down, hands in his pockets, ten-year-old Jeremy wondered if his parents could love him if he was just ordinary, if he never turned into a superstar or a genius the way his brothers had.

He'd walked for miles and had been deep in the woods, sauntering along, trying to guess what his parents would make him try next, and which sport would be the least humiliating, when he heard a rustling sound. *Bird,* he thought. Maybe a squirrel or fox. From the corner of his eye he saw a flash of brown, something much bigger than a squirrel or a fox, something bigger, even, than a man. It was almost bear-size, standing upright on two legs, moving lightly and very fast. What on earth . . . ?

Jeremy started running, sounding like an army on the move as he trampled over sticks and leaped over logs.

The thing up ahead of him was man-shaped, but much larger, with a hat on its head and boots on its feet and some kind of pack on its back, but Jeremy knew that it wasn't a human when it turned sideways and he saw the fur on its face and hands.

The problem was, when Jeremy saw the creature, the creature also saw Jeremy. Its eyes widened in fear, and it started to run. Jeremy gave chase.

"Hey!" he yelled, his breath burning in his chest, as the creature pulled farther and farther ahead. "Hey, wait! Wait! I'm not gonna hurt you!"

Either the creature didn't hear or didn't understand or believe him, because it kept running. Jeremy poured on one last desperate burst of speed, fumbled his phone out of his pocket, poked his passcode onto the touch screen, and began to film the thing that ran on ahead of him.

"Wait!" he yelled. "Wait, please!" The creature never slowed. Jeremy was left with nine seconds of blurry, bouncing footage that showed a large shadowy something slipping through the trees.

"Probably a camper," said Martin when Jeremy, breathless with excitement, finally got his father to look up from his magazine back at home.

"But why would a camper run away from me like that?"

Martin shrugged. "Maybe he was a hunter. Going after deer without a permit."

Jeremy showed his mom the footage. "That's nice, dear," said Suzanne, pouring herself more wine, without looking at all.

Ben, in the middle of a set of jump squats, merely grunted. Noah was the one who talked to him about it . . . but he was far from encouraging.

"Look, J, Bigfoots are a legend," he said.

"I know what I saw," Jeremy repeated. He must have said those words a hundred times since he'd gotten home with his phone footage.

Noah reached over and pulled him into a rare one-armed side hug. "I know it's hard," he began.

Jeremy squirmed away. He hadn't told either of his brothers about the audition disaster. His parents must have filled them in.

"It was real," Jeremy said.

Noah looked dismayed. "Real," Jeremy repeated. "And I'm going to prove it. And you'll be sorry you didn't believe me."

He'd jumped off his brother's bed, grabbed his phone, run to his bedroom, and started googling "Bigfoot" and "sightings" and "Bigfoot is real."

For weeks after his sighting, he'd immersed himself in the online world of Bigfoot hunters, paranormal activities, and UFO sightings. On his travels through the Internet's more obscure byways, he'd found people who believed all kinds of things—that an alien spaceship had crash-landed in New Mexico (and that the aliens from the spaceship were currently running all of the banks and newspapers in America); that the Loch Ness Monster had relocated to the Erie Canal; that NBA TV sent secret, coded messages during its *NBA GameTime* highlights program that ran every morning.

He'd gone to the Standish Public Library to try to find out if anyone had ever seen strange creatures in the local woods, and after the librarian, Ms. Putnam, decided he wasn't a troublemaker, she'd told him about the Standish Historical Society in Mrs. Bradon's garage. Mrs. Bradon had a hundred years' worth of back issues of the *Standish Times* on microfiche, along with a reader that she'd bought when the town library was renovated. Jeremy's goal was to get through ten years of newspapers every day. He was on 1912 when a front-page headline froze him in place, his hand still on the reader's dial, his Bigfoot notebook spread open on his lap.

"Milford Garrison Carruthers and the captive 'Lucille,'"

read the caption underneath the black-and-white drawing of a man standing next to a cringing figure in a cage. Milford Garrison Carruthers had an enormous waxed mustache that turned up at the tips and a watch chain that strained against his belly. He wore a black suit, a striped vest, and a pleased expression as he posed in front of the cowering thing. "The captive 'Lucille'" wore a long dress with a high neck and a bonnet that covered most of her face. Most, but not all of it. The illustration showed that her face was covered in short, dark fur. One furry hand held the handle of a parasol. The other rested lightly on the bars.

Sitting in a corner of Mrs. Bradon's garage, smelling old paper and mildewed lawn furniture and car wax, Jeremy felt his eyes burn as he read the story. "Carruthers, who has downed lions and rhinos in darkest Africa, captured the fearsome creature in the woods surrounding his Standish estate. He claims that the creature—or 'Lucille,' as he has named her—is capable of intelligible speech, and announced plans to sell her to the Sanderson Traveling Circus, where she will be displayed as part of a roster of freaks, including albinos, midgets, giants, Siamese twins, and exotic animals."

Jeremy turned the page to a handbill featuring a drawing of Lucille and inviting people to "come marvel at one of Nature's true Oddities, one of God's Errors, a Freakish Hybrid of Human and Ape."

Back at home, with two copies of the story tucked in his backpack, still feeling hot-eyed and strangely unsettled, Jeremy ate two peanut-butter-honey-banana sandwiches, then sat down in front of his laptop. He'd just started looking up "Milford Garrison Carruthers" and "Standish" and "Bigfoot" and "Lucille" when his screen turned blue. He winced, thinking he'd fried the computer, maybe permanently, when a sentence he hadn't typed appeared in the top right-hand corner. *Greetings, seeker! Want to play a game?* it read.

Jeremy stared at the words, and then shuddered. Maybe he'd been too deeply immersed in the world of space aliens and hidden monsters, but his first thought was that he'd somehow gotten in touch with the ghost of Milford Carruthers . . . or maybe even the ghost of poor Lucille.

The words just hung there, inviting. *Greetings, seeker!* And then another sentence. *Click yes or no.*

When he clicked *yes*, a pattern appeared on his screen: nine dots, in three rows of three. *Connect all nine dots without lifting your pencil using just four lines,* read the instructions.

Jeremy stared, considering. When he touched the cursor, more words appeared: *Think carefully. You will only have one chance.* Jeremy decided to draw out the dots on a piece of paper, tried out different possibilities, and finally realized that the trick was to draw the first line through a row of three vertical dots, then extend it out past the grid before angling it back on the diagonal, to swipe two more dots. Then extending out of the grid again, a horizontal swipe back across, and a diagonal stroke, until the finished puzzle looked a little like the sketch of a bow tie. Four lines, running through all nine dots. "I'm thinking outside the box," he said.

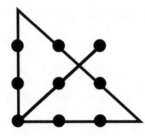

Nice work, flashed on the screen. Then another puzzle appeared, this one a word problem. *A lily pad grows in a pond. Each day the number of lily pads doubles, until, after ten days, the lily pads cover the entire pond. On what day did the lily pads cover half the pond?*

Luckily, Jeremy had heard that one before. If the number doubled each day, then on day nine, half the pond would be covered. Double half, and on day ten the lily pads had taken over. "Day nine," he typed, and wondered if this would actually lead anywhere and who was asking these questions.

What stays in a corner but travels the world? asked the screen.

Jeremy tried to type the riddle into Google and found that whoever he was playing this game with had disabled the feature. It took him two hours, and help from his brother, to come up with the answer: "a stamp." The screen barely paused to congratulate him before spitting out the next riddle.

What starts with the letter t, *is full of tea, and ends with* t?

That one was easy. "Teapot," Jeremy typed. The next riddle appeared.

"What gets wetter and wetter the more it dries?" Jeremy read aloud.

"A towel," called Suzanne, who was working in her office. After he typed in that answer, a rebus appeared.

Jeremy stared, then yelped, "Space invaders!" He typed it in. Another problem popped up.

CORPO**RATE**

"Corporate downsizing?" said Martin, peering at Jeremy's screen on his way to the dinner table with his magazine tucked under his arm. "Hey, kiddo, you've got to come eat." Jeremy typed in the answer, gulped down his chicken and biscuits, and raced back to his computer, which was showing yet another puzzle:

T _ R N

"No *u* turn," Jeremy typed. He was, he thought, getting the hang of it.

After a dozen more riddles and math problems, Jeremy's screen turned blue. *Congratulations!* read a banner on top, as silvery confetti fluttered down. Then a string of numbers appeared, and just like that, his computer was back to normal. "See if they're GPS coordinates," Noah suggested, after Jeremy had puzzled over the digits for hours, trying to see if they were some kind of code, if each number represented a letter that would spell out a word.

Of course Noah was right. The coordinates led to a spot right there in Standish, deep in the forest. Jeremy walked for an hour with his phone set to its compass feature and found, balanced on a tree trunk at the precise coordinates he'd received, a cube composed of brightly colored squares, nine on each side: a Rubik's Cube. When Jeremy solved it, with a final click, the cube twisted into two pieces, and a folded square of paper fell into his hands. It was a note with an address written on it . . . and, on the other side, a copy of the illustration Jeremy had seen in the old newspaper: Milford Garrison Carruthers posing proudly next to the creature in a cage. The hair on the back of his neck stood up as he read the single word handwritten beneath the illustration: "real."

The address turned out to be not far from his school: a single-story bungalow, painted gray with white trim.

Jeremy rang the doorbell. His backpack was full of everything he'd learned or discovered: three Bigfoot notebooks along with printouts of the story about Milford Carruthers; every subsequent newspaper mention of Carruthers, Lucille, or the circus she'd been sold to; and every story about anything—from crimes to Girl

Scout cookouts—that took place in Standish's forests. He had a copy of the footage he'd shot that day in the woods, transferred to a thumb drive, and a copy of the Patterson-Gimlin film, along with a drive containing every tabloid cover that had ever mentioned Bigfoot.

He wasn't sure who, or what, to expect when the door swung open. At first he saw nothing. Then he looked down. A girl sitting in a fancy aerodynamic office chair, with glossy black hair gathered in a ponytail that stuck out of her Red Sox baseball cap, stared up at him. Jeremy saw that she was about his age, and that she did not seem to be entirely pleased.

"You're a kid!" she said.

"So are you!" said Jeremy. He hadn't realized until that moment that he'd half expected whoever had been playing those games with him to be a sixty-year-old man who smelled like cats—not just a grown-up, but a weird grown-up.

"Well," said the girl, without getting up. "You're Jeremy Bigelow, right?" When he nodded, she looked him up and down. "I thought maybe it'd be Noah. We used to go to school together."

Jeremy felt his heart descend toward his knees. Everyone wanted one of his brothers. Nobody ever wanted him.

"But Noah's not into the paranormal," the girl continued.

"And if you were smart enough to solve my riddles, then you're smart enough to be here." She set her hands against the wall, and pushed. The chair spun, then rolled over the smooth wooden floors down the hallway, into the house. "By the way, my father works from home. He's very big and very strong, and very protective of me."

Jeremy raised his hands to show how harmless he was, then realized the girl whose chair was rolling ahead of him couldn't see him.

"I'm Jo," said the girl.

The house was small but airy, with high ceilings, white walls, and pale-green and light-blue furniture. He followed Jo past a living room and a dining room and a kitchen before they arrived at a glassed-in sunroom that had been converted into what looked like Bigfoot Central, or maybe the Pentagon's war room.

"Welcome to the Batcave," Jo said. Jeremy looked around. A detailed map of Standish covered an entire wall and was studded with pushpins in red and green and blue. On the opposite wall, a bookshelf was stocked with everything that had ever been published about Bigfoots. Photographs were layered on a corkboard—color snapshots, movie stills, fuzzy black-and-white images, pictures taken with infrared light that depicted what looked like nothing more than big greenish blobs.

Jo spun her chair around again to face him.

"You're wondering how I found you," she said.

Jeremy had been wondering all kinds of things, including whether Jo was crazy and whether he was safe here. Instead of saying that, though, he just nodded.

"I run Believeinbigfoot.com. Every IP address that visits the site gets a cookie embedded in the hard drive so I can track who's been there."

"Is that legal?" Jeremy wondered.

Jo sounded the tiniest bit smug when she said, "You clicked 'yes' when the site asked your permission to leave it. Anyhow, I set up the cookie to trigger the array when—*if*—anyone ever typed in a string of search words about Standish and Bigfoots and . . ."

"Milford Carruthers," Jeremy finished for her.

Jo nodded. "You were the first person since I started the site to ask questions about Bigfoots here in Standish. Did you see one?" she asked him without preamble.

Jeremy gulped. "One what?"

"A Bigfoot," she said, in a tone as calm as if she'd asked him whether he'd seen a squirrel on his walk over. She must have noticed his shocked expression, because she frowned and said, sounding almost apologetic, "I know that's probably not the preferred term. Probably they call themselves something else." The right half of her mouth quirked upward in a sort of smile. "The differently footed, maybe."

"You think they're real?"

"I know they are," said Jo. She gestured toward the walls—the maps, the books, the photographs. "I know they're real, and I know they're here. Nearby. And I know that I'm going to find them. Now," she said, clapping her hands together, "I want you to tell me everything about your sighting."

"I—I have pictures," Jeremy stammered. He pulled off his backpack and reached for the thumb drive, still trying to make sense of it. Jo held out her hand. Her face was very calm, but her eyes were shining in a way Jeremy had seen in his own mirror. He'd found someone who believed him. More than that, he'd found someone who wasn't looking past him in order to see his brothers or using him to get to Ben or Noah.

Jo didn't care (he hoped) how smart Noah was or how Ben had scored more goals than any soccer player in the town's entire history in his freshman year of high school.

She cared about Bigfoots . . . and, by extension, she cared about Jeremy, too.

CHAPTER 8

Millie

ALL THROUGH SEPTEMBER, MILLIE HAD BEEN permitted precisely an hour of reconnaissance in the morning. After that, Teacher Greenleaf, who was almost as old as Old Aunt Yetta but considerably less indulgent, would call her into class. Millie would scramble down her tree and go to her lessons in the dim little school-burrow, which, like most Yare dwellings, was half underground. When her school day was over, she'd visit Old Aunt Yetta's, where, as part of her Tribe Leader training, she was studying herb lore.

"Ginger," Old Aunt Yetta said, on a rainy afternoon in October. Millie picked up the gnarled beige-colored root.

"For nausea, morning sickness, and . . ." Millie paused, thinking.

"You should know this," Old Aunt Yetta chided.

"Digestion?"

Aunt Yetta nodded, then named another herb. "Black cohosh."

Millie selected a thin branch covered with frilly white blossoms and tiny, round green pods. "Cramps and bone-fret."

"Tincture or tea?"

"Umm . . ."

Old Aunt Yetta sighed. "Nyeh. Smart as you are, you can't do better than this? What will you be doing when I'm gone?"

I'll be gone too, Millie thought. She'd find a way to shed her fur and keep it from coming back. She was sure it could be done. She'd leave the forest and find her real Tribe. She would . . .

"Millie." After all these years, Old Aunt Yetta knew exactly what Millie was thinking. Shaking her head, she set out a small snackle; the crumbly, sweet whole-wheat biscuits that she knew were Millie's favorites; a wheel of goat cheese made from the milk of her own goat, Esmerelda; and a jar of lavender honey. She piled on scones made with chives she'd snipped from her garden; heavy clotted cream; small, sweet apples; dried cherries; and a fun-size Snickers bar as a treat. Like the rest of the Tribe, Old Aunt Yetta was forever trying to fatten Millie up, always keeping a cookie or a sweet in her pocket, putting extra sugar into Millie's tea, extra butter on her bread, and cream on top of her morning oats.

That afternoon Aunt Yetta stuck a small candle into the middle of a seed cake. "Happy Name-Night to you, happy Name-Night to you," she warbled in her off-key, scratchy voice. "I know it isn't until tonight, but I wanted to be wishing you the best." Old Aunt Yetta set a wrapped rectangular box with a bow on top beside Millie's plate. "For when you're done."

The Yare didn't celebrate birthdays. Instead, they honored the seventh day after a baby was born, when the little one received a name. Millie's real name was Millietta, but she'd always been called Millie—or Little Bit or Smallfoot (which was a kind of joke about how the No-Furs called the Tribe Bigfoots), or Little Silver, because of her fur.

Millie smiled and clapped. "Thank you."

"Nyebbeh," said Aunt Yetta, which, in that instance, meant, "You're welcome, even though I am still a little upset with you."

Millie tucked in, Old Aunt Yetta watching with approval. "Didn't you eat your snackle at school?"

Millie shrugged. The truth was, she'd been thinking so much about the noise and bustle across the lake that she'd barely remembered to nibble the cheese and crackers Teacher Greenleaf had served.

"Were you daydreaming?" asked Old Aunt Yetta, who was familiar with all of Millie's bad habits.

Millie sighed. "In a No-Fur book I am reading, I learned about elections. Do you know that the No-Furs pick their Leaders, and it doesn't even matter much what clan they are from?"

"What are they calling their Leaders?"

Millie crunched a bite of apple. "Presiment?"

"President," Old Aunt Yetta corrected her.

"The name is not mattering," said Millie. "You could be anyone, from any clan! As long as you are good and fair and the No-Furs like you, then you can be their Leader!" She kicked at the wooden chair with the heel of her small foot. It barely made a sound, which only made Millie madder. "And then the No-Fur who doesn't want to be the Leader can go and do singing!"

"Oh, Millie." Old Aunt Yetta smoothed the soft silvergray fur on Millie's forehead. Millie ate another scone.

The breeze that had been rustling the tree branches died down, and in the quiet Millie and Old Aunt Yetta heard a burst of laughter from across the lake.

"Will my father do the Mailing tomorrow?" Millie asked, her tone casual and her eyes on her plate.

Old Aunt Yetta sighed. She knew that Millie's interest in the Mailing, and the town of Standish and the No-Furs who lived there, was anything but casual.

"How did we get the Mailing box?" Millie asked.

"We did it on-the-line," said Old Aunt Yetta, in a tone that let Millie know not to pursue the subject.

"But someone must have gone to the posting office. Someone must have had to talk to the No-Furs and get the key, because they couldn't have mailed us a key if there wasn't a box yet to mail it to." Millie sat back smiling triumphantly. "Nyeh!"

"Millie . . ." Now Old Aunt Yetta was practically groaning.

Millie raised her head. Her eyes shone in her furry face. "I bet there's a way for us to un-fur ourselves and go out into the world. I bet my father . . ."

"Millie," said Old Aunt Yetta, speaking in a sharp tone she rarely used with her young friend. "That's enough."

"There must be a way, and if there is, I will find it."

Old Aunt Yetta stifled another groan.

"So how is it done?" Millie asked. Her face was alive with excitement. "Is it shaving?" Millie had actually tried that on her own, but the single old razor that she'd found hadn't done much more than trim her fur short, leaving her with an oddly patchy look that the other littlies, especially Tulip, had found endlessly amusing.

"Shaving does not work," Old Aunt Yetta said.

"Why? Why does it not work?"

"Because the fur comes back."

"Why? How fast? And when we are un-furred, do we look like them?"

"No," Old Aunt Yetta said, her voice stern. "No, we do not."

Millie didn't believe her. She'd made a careful study of herself in the single mirror in her family's home. With her head-hair slicked back, she looked almost like a regular No-Fur girl, like someone who could wear regular-girl clothing and pass in the regular-girl world.

But she knew when she'd pushed hard enough. She sat up straight, brushing crumbs out of her face-fur and piling them neatly on her napkin.

"Shmeh," said Old Aunt Yetta, which was a polite Yare word for "Let's stop discussing this uncomfortable subject." "Open your giftie."

Millie unwrapped the box and clapped in delight when she saw it was a collection of six episodes of *Friends*. "Can we watch a nepisode?"

"Just one," Old Aunt Yetta said. "And it is 'episode.'"

Millie beamed, jumped up from her chair, and flung her arms around Old Aunt Yetta's waist. Old Aunt Yetta made sure the door was latched and no one was nearby, and Millie settled into a pile of cushions on the floor and sang and clapped along as the theme song began. *"So no one told you life was gonna be this way . . ."* It was true, she thought . . . but it was also true that no one had told her that her life would be this way forever. She could change it; she could take control of her own destiny, could learn the secrets that would let her escape her little village and go out into the great wide world.

"Millie."

At midnight Millie opened her eyes. Her parents were standing by the side of her bed, smiling. Her father's arms were filled with wrapped gifties. Her mother carried Millie's favorite carrot cake with cream-cheese frosting, with twelve lit candles standing in a ring around its edge.

"Happy Name-Night!" her parents whispered, and Millie beamed and gave her parents the biggest hug she could.

She blew out the candles, and her father handed her the first box, wrapped in pink-and-white paper, with a card from Amazon tucked under the ribbon.

Millie's eyes widened. Carefully she removed the paper and the card and tucked them away for safekeeping. Then she opened the box and gasped in delight. Nestled in a cloud of tissue paper was a pair of sparkly red shoes, No-Fur shoes, with metal buckles. "Like in the movie!" she said.

"Just so," rumbled Maximus. (Her parents knew she'd seen *The Wizard of Oz*, because the previous winter, during a blizzard that had kept the Tribe inside for days, Old Aunt Yetta had arranged a screening and had served popcorn and hot chocolate as the littlies snuggled in piles of pillows and blankets on her floor. Tulip, Millie remembered, had refused to even watch, and Florrie had cried at the green-faced No-Fur pretending to be a witch.)

Millie swung her legs out of bed. They dangled above the floor as she slipped on the shoes, which were the perfect size for her little feet. Next she unwrapped a heavy, beautifully bound collection of Grimm's fairy tales, a boxed set of Anne of Green Gables books, and a dozen ribbons in pinks and yellows and blues that she could clip into her head-hair.

There was a box of chocolate-covered cherries, a box of sea-salt caramels, and a single, slightly battered video-cassette of season ten of *Friends* that her parents told her sternly she was only to watch with Old Aunt Yetta and was never to mention to Tulip or any of the other Yare.

"I promise, I promise!" Millie said. Her father hugged her, and Septima smiled her shy smile, with one hand, as always, over her mouth. (Millie suspected that someone had told her mother at a very early age that she had ugly teeth, because every time she smiled, Septima's hand would always wander up to cover her lips.)

Millie walked between her parents down the slope that led to the edge of the lake, for the ritual Name-Night dunking . . . and there, feeling her happiness swell like a bubble inside of her, Millie started to sing: "Happy Name-Night to me, happy Name-Night to me, happy NAME-Night, dear MILL-EEEE . . ."

"Shh!" said Maximus, looking around to make sure they were alone, as Septima pinched Millie's lips together gently but firmly.

"When you are Leader," she began, "you must be setting the example, Millie. You know how voices carry across the water."

"I wasn't even being loudness." Millie struggled not

to sigh, hating the petulant, babyish sound of her voice. Hating, more than that, the constant necessity for quiet, endless quiet, even with the Tribe's village in the center of an untouched forest far from the nearest human home, with thick woods on three sides and a wide lake on the fourth.

"Happy Name-Night," said Maximus, and handed her a penny. "Do your wishing!"

Millie held the penny tightly and closed her eyes as she waded into the water until she was submerged. *I wish,* she thought, as hard as she could, *I wish I could climb into a boat and paddle myself away.*

She let the penny sink to the bottom of the lake and climbed out of the water, shaking her fur briskly, then trotting to her parents, who'd been watching from the shore. Not many Yare liked the water—their muscular bodies and dense fur didn't make it easy for them to float or swim—but Millie had always loved the lake.

"Little dreamer," said Septima, bending to give her daughter a towel and a kiss, and her father called her his heart's delight, which made Millie's eyes prickle and her throat get tight. *I will be good,* she promised herself. *I'll do what they tell me, I'll be who they want.*

But early the next morning, Millie could hear the

No-Furs on the opposite side of the lake. Splashes and shrieks of laughter, clapping and shouting and songs. She scrambled up the Lookout Tree and through her binoculars saw that they'd tied a rope to a tall tree of their own, and they were taking turns swinging out over the water before jumping in. It was just too tempting . . .

So at lunch she sidled over to Jacobus, who was two years younger than she was. Jacobus was a hulking young Yare with enormous shoulders and hands, and curly reddish-brown fur.

"Happy Name-Day," he said, reaching out to hold both of Millie's hands in his, the ritual greeting the Yare gave one another on special occasions. "Do you have any cake left over?"

She handed him a wedge of carrot cake, then said, as casually as she could, "You are knowing where the canoe is, right?"

Before Jacobus could answer, Tulip walked over to join them. The fur around her eyes and ears was looking even darker. "Why are you asking about canoes?"

"Why are you asking why I'm asking?" Millie responded.

Tulip looked smug. "You want to go over to where the No-Furs are."

Millie straightened to her full height, which took

her to Jacobus's chest and Tulip's shoulder. "What if I do? I'm supposed to be spying. I could gather valuable information."

"Like what?" sniffed Tulip. "The words to more of their songs?"

In for a penny, in for a pounding, Millie thought. That was what Old Aunt Yetta said. "It's important for the Tribe to be knowing what the No-Furs are up to. You could come with me!" she offered.

Jacobus stepped backward, away from Millie, and Tulip flinched.

"We don't even have to go all the way to shore; we can just get close enough to see what all the noise is," Millie said.

Jacobus shook his head with his brow-fur bristling and his expression grave. "Millie," he said, "you know we can't go near them."

"They won't see us!" she said. "It'll be dark, and we'll be in a boat, on the water."

"Nyebbeh," Tulip said, and went back to the classroom— to tattle, Millie thought. Jacobus continued walking backward, with the remnants of Millie's cake looking very small in his hands. "I should tell your parents what you're saying."

She grabbed his arm-fur and tugged it hard. "Nyebbeh! Nugget! No!"

"But you can't go." He crouched down and stared into her eyes. "You have to promise you won't."

"I won't," she grumbled.

"Remember Cassoundra," he said.

"I do," she said, feeling miserable. Every Yare remembered Cassoundra, the only Yare to ever appear—accidentally, of course—in a No-Fur movie. Cassoundra, whose Tribe lived in California, had been filmed by No-Furs after she'd wandered near their campsite. She was the reason modern-day No-Furs had even a vague idea of what the Yare looked like and where they lived. As a result of Cassoundra's mistake, her clan had to leave its encampment where they'd lived for two hundred years, and Cassoundra had been cast out of the Tribe, her feet set on the road. Her name was the one the Yare used when they wanted to tell their children how dire the consequences of discovery could be, to scare them into good behavior, or silence.

Jacobus shuffled closer to Millie and whispered in her ear a name that was hardly ever spoken out loud. "Remember Demetrius."

Millie shuddered. Demetrius was the name of her

father's twin brother. Demetrius had been curious, like Millie ("That's where she gets it," Septima was fond of remarking, usually with an exasperated look toward her spouse). He too liked to climb up trees to spy on the campers across the lake; he too had been heard talking about what it would be like to take a canoe in the dead of night and paddle over to their side.

Most of all—worst of all—Demetrius was a student of history. He'd read the same books as Millie. He knew that the Yare and the No-Furs had once lived together side by side, and he believed that if the No-Furs just got to know the Yare, if they realized that their differences were mostly external—a matter of hair and size—then they would welcome them, and the Yare and the No-Furs could live as friends once again.

His parents tried to stop him, Maximus had told Millie, with a grave expression and his deep voice even deeper than usual. They punished him for spying; they bribed him with treats and gifts; they begged and pleaded and explained, over and over, how risky it was. But when he was sixteen, Demetrius disappeared. A canoe was found missing, along with a packsack and most of his clothes and books. He'd left a note saying that he loved his parents and his brother but that he was going to see the world.

"Is he dead?" Millie had asked, her lips trembling, her mouth dry.

Maximus had given her a sober look. "We will never know," he said . . . and that, somehow, seemed even worse than having an uncle who'd died.

"Millie," said Jacobus.

Millie looked at him. "I remember what I'm taught." Her little hands had curled into fists, and she could feel her silvery fur bristling, making her look like an indignant porcupine. "I know, I know, I know!"

All through her lessons, as the day dragged on, Millie could hear splashes and shouts and laughter. Even after Teacher Greenleaf looked at her sternly and pulled the curtains across the window, Millie could hear them. It was all too much . . . and, two days after her Name-Night, she couldn't resist the temptation any longer.

CHAPTER 9

Alice

BETWEEN DAILY CONVERSATION AND MORNING Nutrition, Alice found out that the Experimental Center's new arrival's name was Jessica Jarvis, and she was coming to school so late because she'd either been a guest at or a model in Fashion Week in New York City. Jessica's father was a famous designer. Her mother had been his favorite model, and Jessica was their only, beloved child. She'd been sent to the Experimental Center because of its extremely forgiving policies about "off-campus learning opportunities."

"Also," Taley said, "I thinkbd they givde her class creditb for modeling."

On their way to their first learning session, Lori had

made an introduction. "You're both from New York City, Alice. You and Jessica should have a lot to talk about!" she said. The sunshine glistened on her big front teeth, and Alice could see the faint, downy mustache on her upper lip. From the way Jessica was smirking, Alice suspected that the other girl could too.

Alice extended her hand, and Jessica gave Alice her own hand, as limp as a plastic bag full of warm water. "What neighborhood are you from?" Alice asked automatically— the thing every New Yorker asked his or her fellows when encountering them elsewhere in the world.

Jessica pushed the words "Upper East Side" through her barely parted lips, with her torso tilted backward like she couldn't wait to get away from Alice. Her voice, unlike Riya's quiet tones and Taley's nasal honk, was lovely, low and sweet, like she'd taken singing lessons or had a secret career as a news anchor. "And you?" she asked, because Lori was still there.

"Eighty-Ninth Street and Fifth Avenue," said Alice, and was gratified to see Jessica's eyebrow give an incremental twitch of surprise, probably because Alice came from a neighborhood that Jessica regarded as acceptable.

"You'll help Alice feel welcome in our community?" Lori asked as Jessica retrieved her hand.

"Of course!" said Jessica.

Lori gave a little skipping twirl of delight before a loud, grating noise distracted her. Across from the soccer fields, one of the learning guides had rigged a blender to a bicycle with a plan of getting the kids to pedal, using their own energy to turn basil and garlic and pine nuts and olive oil into pesto. Except the guide had failed to put the lid on the blender before the pedaling commenced, and three learners and a half dozen nearby trees had gotten sprayed with garlicky green goo. Lori ran over to help, and Jessica flounced away in a swirl of shiny hair and a cloud of forbidden aerosol hairspray.

That night, when Alice went back to the Ladybug cabin, her bed had been stripped. Her fluffy white comforter and crisply pillowcased pillows had all been dumped in a heap on the floor. Her clothes had been pulled out of the cubbies and tossed on top of the bedding, and the bed that had been hers was now made up with a pink flowered quilt and peach satin pillows. Alice bit her lip, resisting the impulse to return the favor, to yank off all the invading sweet-smelling peachy-pink stuff and toss it on the floor . . . or better yet, into the lake. She knew what this meant. She'd hoped that maybe the Center wouldn't be like her other schools. Taley and Riya weren't friends, but they weren't awful, and she had her lessons with Kate. Plus, twice in the week before, she'd seen one of the eighth-grade boys on an early-morning run of his own. The second time he'd even waved at her. But now the turning point had come, the moment where the Experimental Center would change into the same kind of torture chamber that every one of her other schools had been.

"Sorry, I need the bottom bunk," Jessica said. "Vertigo. Oh, and I needed more space in the bathroom, so I put your"—she paused just long enough for the silence to stretch to an insulting length—"*things* underneath the sink."

Instead of complaining, Alice quietly went about making the top bed and putting her belongings away in the corresponding cubbies. There'd been a Jessica at each of her previous schools. Fighting with that girl—whether her name was Miranda or Olivia or Sophie or Sally— never did any good. Neither did telling the teachers. You just kept your head down, stayed out of their way, and hoped they found other targets.

Unfortunately, Jessica seemed to decide that tormenting Alice was her personal mission . . . and it was work she took seriously. In the mornings, when Alice came back from the forest, Jessica was in the shower, and she stayed there, filling the room with steam and the cloying scent of peach body wash, using up all of the hot water as Alice, muddy and miserable, brushed her teeth and waited.

"Privacy!" Jessica would sing, slamming the bathroom door and locking the other three girls out.

At meals she would sit next to the basketball-shorts boys, giggling and whispering. The giggles and whispers always stopped when Alice passed them, then resumed, much more loudly, as she walked away.

During learning sessions Jessica would tilt her head adorably and say, "I'm sorry, what was that?" whenever Alice gave an answer or read out loud. "Can you speak up and stop mumbling, please? I really want to hear what you have to say."

Within a week of her arrival, Jessica had assembled her clique: two eighth-grade girls, Cara and Christy, and three of the long-basketball-shorts-wearing boys, a clump that Alice thought of as the Steves (only one of the boys—the one who'd waved at her—was named Steve, but they all looked and dressed the same, and Alice had never managed to learn their names). Cara was a tall girl with long legs and fine features whose parents were actors in Los Angeles. Christy was plain and quiet to the point of invisibility. Taley's theory, which Alice had overheard her explain to Riya, was that the glamorous Jessica and Cara kept Christy around because she made them feel pretty and because she paid for everything with the generous allowance her parents sent.

Alice supposed she should be grateful that Jessica was hardly ever in their cabin, unless she was monopolizing the shower or changing her clothes. All three girls had learned not to try to get near the bunk's single mirror when Jessica was using it or to complain about how her various hair-styling implements took up all four of the electrical outlets in the cabin.

"Silence, ladies," Jessica would say. Somehow, the word "silence" sounded worse than "shut up," and "ladies" sounded worse than "losers." Jessica's disdain could have been the thing that brought the girls together, united against a common enemy, but Jessica cleverly made sure that didn't happen.

"I don't think fencing's a weird hobby at all," she'd said on her second day at school, with her hand on a confused Riya's shoulder. "I know some people"—she cut her eyes at Alice—"think it means you're a dangerous sociopath who wants to stab someone for real, but not all of us agree."

Riya had snatched up her helmet and stalked away, and when Alice had tried to explain, Riya interrupted her with a clipped "It's fine."

"Justdb ignoredb her," Taley said. Alice tried . . . but a week into Jessica's reign, just as Alice was getting used to the new reality, everything changed.

"Alice," Jessica purred as she flounced into the cabin one day after lunch.

Alice was so startled to hear her name coming out of her bunkmate's mouth that at first she assumed she'd misheard. It wasn't until Jessica tapped her shoulder, making an impatient face, and said, "Earth to Alice, come in, Alice," that Alice realized that Jessica was, in fact, talking to her.

"Do you want to borrow something?" Whatever Jessica wanted, Alice decided, she would let her have. It would be easier than fighting.

Jessica laughed, shaking her head. "No, no. I was just wondering if you wanted to sit with us tonight at . . . um . . ." She wrinkled her nose charmingly. "What are we calling it now?"

"Evening Nutrition." Alice felt like she was watching herself in a movie, as Jessica leaned toward her, smelling like apricots from the body spray she'd just applied. "And no thanks."

"I think Steven likes you."

Alice felt her body flush with pleasure, even as she wondered about how a boy who'd never spoken to her could like her, and which boy Steven was. From her spot at her sewing machine, Taley was watching with interest, her watery hazel eyes magnified behind her glasses. Riya, who was slipping leggings on underneath her skirt, had frozen in the act. As Jessica waited, Taley began shaking her head, silently but firmly, while mouthing the word "no."

Alice felt a flare of annoyance. She sat near Taley and Riya at most meals, but Riya usually just talked about fencing, and Taley spent most of her time cross-examining Kate about possible allergens in the food. Alice was sure they were just tolerating her, enduring her company because they knew Lori would fuss, or maybe even arrange a lecture on "A mind-set of kindness," if she saw a learner sitting alone . . . and there'd definitely never been a boy who'd wanted to join them.

"Come on," Jessica said, and laughed her chiming laugh. "It's no big deal! He wants to get to know you!"

Of course, Alice was suspicious as to why a girl who'd done nothing but ignore her and tease her suddenly wanted to be her friend. But Jessica was dazzling—there was no other word for it. It was almost as if she exerted her own gravity, and Alice was powerless to resist. And Alice wanted so badly to believe that it could be true; that this beautiful girl could like her; that a boy liked her too.

"Okay," she said. Jessica beamed and clapped her hands,

a gesture Alice remembered her own mother making, usually when Alice emerged from one of her weekly trips to the salon with the Mane blown perfectly straight.

That night Alice was the one monopolizing the mirror and the shower, as she used her own body wash (scented with lemons and sage) and attempted to style her hair. Taley and Riya watched this with expressions of sadness (Taley) and skepticism (Riya).

"Alice," Riya finally said. "Jessica Jarvis is not a good person."

Alice felt her shoulders stiffen. "At least she wants me to be around," she said.

Riya and Taley exchanged a glance.

"We wantb you aroundb," said Taley.

Alice kept her eyes on her reflection, thinking that it couldn't be true. "If you did," she said, "then you would have invited me to go into town with you. Or you would have asked me to meditate with you . . . or play chess . . . or something!"

In the mirror's reflection, Alice could see Riya and Taley exchange another look.

"We didb invite youdb," Taley said. "You always said 'no.'"

"You could invite us to do things with you," Riya pointed out. "We could get up in the morning and go for a run."

Alice swallowed hard. She knew this was true. They had asked—or at least, they had during her first weeks at the Center—but she'd turned them down with a curt "No thank you" because she knew that they were only being polite. She felt her face getting hot underneath her neatly combed hair. As she watched, a curl sprang free and bounced against her forehead, and another one boinged against the back of her neck.

"I have to go," she muttered, and pushed her way past them. She walked quickly to the Lodge, where Jessica and her friends were waiting, as happy and welcoming as if they were throwing a party and Alice was their guest of honor.

The next week was the best time that Alice could remember, at the Center or at any of her schools, and maybe even in her entire life. Jessica and Cara and Christy were all so nice, so sweet and funny, treating Alice like a cross between a little sister and a posable doll with hair you could arrange in six different styles. They asked about New York City, wondering if Alice knew this girl from Swifton or that boy from the Atwater School. They never made her feel bad if she hadn't been to a shop or a restaurant that Jessica mentioned or hadn't seen a movie that Cara knew. They swept Alice into their embrace, lending her whatever clothes they had that fit; curling and braiding and straightening her hair, exclaiming over how thick and shiny it was; plucking her eyebrows and painting her nails; laughing at her observations about the Center and its inhabitants. The meaner Alice's comments were, the more they'd laugh. When Alice said she sometimes thought of Taley as Jack the Dripper, because of her runny nose, they had shrieked in approval, and when she shared her observation about Phil and Lori resembling an exclamation point and a period, Jessica had actually applauded.

At night they hung out in the eighth-grade girls' cabin, where she and Jessica and Christy and Cara would slouch on the top bunk with their legs dangling over the side, listening to music on Jessica's phone and discussing their main topics of interest: the Experimental Center and how awful it was, the Steves and how cute they were. (Alice had shyly confessed that she just thought of the boys as the Steves, and Jessica had been so delighted that she'd decreed that, from that moment forward, the boys would be known only as the Steves.)

Jessica had been at the Center for its entire four-year existence, and knew all the history. She remembered when Lori and Phil had tried to ban makeup on the grounds that cosmetics represented women's "capitulation to patriarchal, capitalistic beauty standards," and how Jessica and two other girls, now graduated, had talked them out of it by arguing that a ban would curtail girls' creativity and self-expression. Jessica remembered the Great Gluten War of the previous year, and the time Lori and Phil decided that keeping score during sports was "hurtful to young learners' self-esteem."

"So of course the Center got kicked out of the league," Jessica said. "Which is why our teams just scrimmage each other."

Best of all, though—better than having friends to hang out with at meals and talk with during free time—were their late-night adventures. When the rest of the Center was asleep, the girls slipped out of their cabins and down to the lake to go night swimming. Even in the first week of October the water was warm and silky, and the darkness disguised Alice's despised body, her thighs and her belly and her enormous hands. Swimming underwater, skimming over the soft sand of the lake bed, with her hair actually looking pretty as it streamed out behind her, Alice could almost imagine Steve's eyes on her, could almost believe that a boy thought she was beautiful . . . especially because one of the Steves, the boy whose name actually was Steve, seemed to go out of his way to talk to her. At dinner he'd sit next to her. When she made jokes, he'd smile. Even though they'd only exchanged two sentences—"Please pass the milk" and "Here you go"—Alice imagined that she could feel him watching her, in the mornings when she went running, then at night when she swam.

True, Alice had heard a few conversations stop when she got to the table, had heard a few bursts of unpleasant-sounding laughter after she got up to get more hummus or more loaf. Her body would tense at the sound, the hair on the back of her neck prickling as she saw the Steves and Jessica and Cara and Christy with their heads all together, whispering. She told herself not to be suspicious. The girls had been nothing but nice to her, and when she came back to the table, Steve would scoot over and pat the empty space on the bench beside him. She stuck by Jessica's side, avoiding the cabin, avoiding Taley and Riya, who, clearly, were jealous of Alice's new friendship, when they tried to warn her away.

"They're justb usingdb you," Taley would say, giving Alice her most sincere look, with her eyes watering from whatever pollen was currently in the air, and her hands full of whatever dress she was making.

"Maybe you're just jealous that they're not using you," Alice finally muttered. There was a loud noise as Riya, on the top bunk, slammed her thick *On Fencing* book shut and jumped from the bed to the floor.

"Taley is not jealous," she said, each word precise and clipped and clear. "Neither am I. Those girls are shallow and mean, and they don't want to be your friends."

"How do you know?" Alice's face was hot, and she felt like she was swelling with embarrassment and anger, her body growing even bigger than it normally was. "Is it so crazy that there are people in this world who actually want to be my friend?"

"It's not crazy," said Riya. "But it's not those girls."

"Then why?" Alice asked. "If they don't want to be my friend, then why do they want to spend time with me? They like me," she added before Taley or Riya could offer a theory. "Sorry if you two find that so hard to believe." She tossed her hair like Jessica did—or, rather, she tried to, except when Jessica tossed her hair it gave kind of a silky shiver, whereas Alice's toss just sent her heavy braid whacking into her back.

This is real, she told herself. Finally, after years of misery, she'd found the place where she fit, the people who could see beyond her exterior, past the giant hands and wild hair, could see that, inside, she was funny, clever, and beautiful. Or maybe not beautiful, but at least the same as they were ... and she wasn't going to let Taley and Riya mess it up.

Two weeks after her first evening meal with Jessica and her friends, Alice was sitting between Cara and

Christy at the table, when Jessica beckoned them all close. "We should go skinny-dipping," Jessica said, her eyebrows arched and her cheeks flushed.

Alice felt icy prickles along her skin. She swallowed hard. So far, she'd always worn a bathing suit, a modest one-piece with a long-sleeved rash guard on top, when they went in the water.

"Don't worry!" Jessica giggled. "It's completely dark . . . and it feels amazing. Have you ever been skinny-dipping?"

Alice had, with her granny, in Cape Cod. She remembered how free she'd felt, how she'd let the waves toss her, pretending that she was a mermaid with an elegant silvery tail and that she could escape to the depths of the ocean and live in a castle of coral and sand.

"I don't know . . . ," murmured Christy.

Jessica pouted. "Oh, come on. Don't be a party pooper. Alice?" Jessica's face lit up. "Are you in?"

"I'm in," Alice said, and, once again, Jessica applauded.

That night Alice followed the other girls to the edge of the lake. They hid behind trees to strip, and left their clothes folded neatly on the towels they'd brought, in a pile at the water's edge. On Jessica's command they dashed, giggling, through the darkness and into the lake.

It was a cloudy, moonless night, the darkness of the

sky and the water so complete that Alice could hardly see her own arms and legs underneath her. She felt like she had finally achieved her goal of invisibility, and it was as glorious as she imagined.

Floating on her back, staring up at the sky, Alice felt beautiful and happy and free. *This is all I ever wanted,* she thought dreamily, hearing splashing and the sound of her friends' laughter. *I will never be any happier than this.*

Then the laughter took on a nasty edge. Alice flipped over, peering toward the shore. She heard the sound of splashing and whispers and running. She started stroking swiftly toward the Center, just in time to see a fully clothed Steve—she couldn't tell which one—scoop up her towel and her clothes and vanish into the woods.

"Hey," she called. She could hear the Steves laughing. The girls were laughing too. "You guys! Hey!"

Nobody came. They were waiting for her, Alice realized miserably as she dog-paddled in chest-deep water, making sure no one could see. Probably they had a camera or a cell phone. They'd take pictures of her, and they'd put them online or email them to every kid at the Center or—

"Alice!" That was Jessica, her cultured voice sounding cruel. "Oh, A-lice! You can't stay in there forever. Come out. We'll give you your clothes."

"Why'd you take them?" Alice called.

More laughter. More rustling. More whispers. She thought of Taley's sad looks, the speech that Riya had made. They'd been right. Maybe they hadn't known the details, but they'd known that Jessica and her friends had been planning something, and they'd tried to tell Alice, but Alice hadn't listened. She had been so caught up in the clearly ridiculous fantasy that a girl like Jessica would actually want to be her friend, so desperate to believe, that she'd ignored the truth. Girls like that never wanted to be friends with big, ugly weirdos like her.

The good thing about crying in the water was that there was no clothing to soak. The tears rolled right off your cheeks and plopped into the lake. Alice paddled and cried, silently, so hard that she got the hiccoughs, for so long that she was surprised she had any tears left.

She could wait until morning, when Jessica and her crew would have to go to Mother Tree. Except if she did that, then maybe everyone in the school would see her in the water. Or she could make a break for it—cover herself up as best she could and run as fast as possible.

"Al-ice . . . ," Jessica was taunting. "Come out, come out, wherever you are!"

Alice flipped onto her belly, swam to the shallows, and

finger-walked to the very edge of the shore. Scooping up fistfuls of silty sand, she slathered herself from shoulders to thighs with pine-needle-studded lake mud and raked her fingers through her hair, pulling it as straight as possible, to cover as much of her chest as it could. She tried her hardest, layering leaves and pine needles onto her skin, trying to make sure that she'd covered as much of her body as possible. Then, teeth chattering, face still wet with tears, she hauled herself up and out of the water, and ignoring the burst of laughter and the flash of someone's camera, she hunched over, and ran as fast as she could back to her cabin.

She was shaking all over by the time she arrived, filthy and soaking and trying not to cry or wake up her roommates. But, of course, Riya was awake, saber flashing as she fenced with an imaginary opponent, and Taley woke up as soon as Alice came in the door.

"Oh my goodness," Taley said as Alice hurried past her. "What happened?"

"Alice, are you all right?" Riya asked.

"Leave me alone!" Alice said, turning on the shower and yanking the curtain shut, too ashamed to look at them and see pity on their faces, or hear them say *I told you so*.

CHAPTER 10

Millie

THE FINAL EPISODE OF SEASON NINE OF *THE Next Stage*, scheduled to air on a Wednesday night, was the culmination of twelve weeks of competition, during which forty-eight competitors had been whittled down to just two acts. During the finale, the two remaining contenders would perform in a "head-to-head battle of epic proportions"—at least, according to the show's head judge, Benjamin Burton.

One finalist was a singer, a woman named Darcy Baker who looked like a plump and somewhat frumpy grandmother, with oversize eyeglasses and fine white hair in a bun . . . until she opened her mouth, and it sounded like she'd swallowed a choir of angels. Darcy, who was Millie's favorite, was up against Los Kicks, a troop of precision pop-and-lock dancers who'd do things like turn their bodies into human rocking chairs for one another to sit on, and form and reform elaborate and precarious pyramids and patterns to the tune of Top 40 music.

For years Old Aunt Yetta had taped each Wednesday-night show, and then, on Thursdays and Fridays, provided she did well with her lessons, Millie would be permitted to watch an hour of the show at a time. But the grand finale was three hours long, featuring every previous grand-prize winner in the show's entire history, plus a performance by Danna de la Cruz, Millie's absolute favorite singer in the world. Millie knew that there was no way she'd be able to wait until Thursday to see the first hour and all the way until Saturday or Sunday or even the following week to find out who'd won.

For days leading up to the finale she'd been thinking nonstop, her mind churning up solutions, all of them ultimately impossible or flawed. She'd considered putting a potion of slippery willow bark into Old Aunt Yetta's tea and watching the show while her friend slept. But sleeping aids were risky, and Aunt Yetta's heart wasn't strong. She'd thought about inventing some emergency to call

Old Aunt Yetta away, but for that to work she would need a partner, and she knew that none of the other littlies would help, or could fake illness convincingly. There were no other television sets in the Yare village . . . but, of course, Millie knew who had television sets. The No-Furs did. They had sets in every room of their houses; they had phones that showed programs and movies on their tiny screens; they'd even, she'd heard, invented eyeglasses with built-in displays so you could watch anything you wanted just by blinking a request.

The No-Fur school across the lake had at least one set. Millie had seen its bluish glow coming through the windows of the big building on top of the hill. Those kids would be watching the finale; she was sure of it. She just needed to figure out how to get there and how to disguise herself, so that if anyone spotted her, tucked into the shadows underneath the window, she'd look like just another No-Fur girl.

The night before the finale, she was still trying to figure it out. After her lessons, she joined Old Aunt Yetta in the garden, wearing a wide-brimmed hat that Septima insisted on, so the sun wouldn't make her silver-gray fur any lighter than it already was. Millie pulled weeds without being asked, and when she was sure Old Aunt Yetta was listening, Millie ran her hand through the fur on her head and sighed.

Old Aunt Yetta raised an eyebrow.

Millie pulled a few more weeds, then asked, "If a Yare was wanting to get more fur, is there a way to do that?"

Old Aunt Yetta's face was sympathetic as she patted Millie's back. "There are things we can try. Rosemary, pine pitch, and dried dandelion greens . . ." Tapping her finger on her lip, clicking her tongue against the roof of her mouth, Old Aunt Yetta, Millie knew, was lost to the world, imagining potions and powders, different ingredients and what each would do.

"What if I was wanting my fur to change color? Could I kill it?" Millie asked.

"Dye it," Old Aunt Yetta corrected. "And no one's ever having success with that. Yare have tried everything when they start to go gray. Boiled walnut shells, crushed quartz, soapstone . . ."

"How about making fur go away?" Millie's eyes were on the pumpkin vines, her voice blamelessly casual. She knew there was a way . . . she just had to get her friend to tell her how.

Old Aunt Yetta's head swiveled, and her golden eyes narrowed.

"Millie Maximus," she asked, "what are you playing at?"

"Nothing!" said Millie. "Nothing! I was just having some curiosity. My fur is so strange. I thought maybe if I got rid of it and started over, it would grow back regular. Regular brown." She made her face sad and her eyes despondent and gave her lower lip a quiver. It was an expression that would have torn at the heart of any observer less familiar with Millie's tricks and poses.

Unfortunately, Old Aunt Yetta was very familiar with Millie's tricks and poses. Bending down, she put her hands on Millie's shoulders and looked her sternly in the eye. "You are planning for something," she said as Millie squirmed and began to stammer out denials. "I don't know what it is, but I know you're having a plan . . . and I won't help you. It would break your mother's heart."

Millie squirmed out of Old Aunt Yetta's grasp. "But when," she demanded, "do I get to mind my own happiness? When do I get to be me?" Then Millie remembered her mission and made her expression mournful once again. "I mean," she said, with a catch in her voice, "if I was only looking like the other littlies, I'd feel more like I belonged here."

Old Aunt Yetta studied her carefully. Millie held her breath. Finally, Old Aunt Yetta sighed and said, "If darker fur is really what you want, then maybe there's a way."

Millie tried to keep her face grave and her feet from skipping as she followed Old Aunt Yetta into her kitchen. A row of ancient, hand-bound books lined the shelf above the old iron stove, their heavy parchment pages covered from top to bottom and left to right with different handwriting in different colors of faded ink. Antidotes and salves and teas and decoctions, handed down from Healers over generations, all of them in the books.

Clicking her tongue, Old Aunt Yetta took a book off the shelf, pulled on her spectacles, and began to read. After a minute Millie helped herself to a volume. She flipped through it until she saw an illustration of a Yare giving birth, and put it back, wincing. The next book was all about first aid: bee stings and snake bites and how to set broken bones. Finally, in a third book, she found pages of scribbles, lists of ingredients, crossed-out additions and footnotes, taped scraps of paper, and—she felt her heart skip—drawings of fur, thick fur, patchy fur, gray fur, brown fur, and even a full-grown Yare with no fur at all.

Millie ran her fingers over the hand-drawn picture, feeling her heart beat faster. It was an adult male Yare, dressed in human clothing, his face completely smooth.

He wore a hat on his head, leather gloves on his hands, and high boots covering his feet . . . but other than those additions, he looked just like a No-Fur man—a very big and tall one. Millie studied the list of ingredients written alongside the picture, her heart sinking with each thing she'd never heard of or had no idea how to obtain: dandelion leaves, lavender oil, essence of mint, a jigger of brandy, crushed snail shell (one medium or two small), three spider legs . . .

"Beetroot," Old Aunt Yetta murmured, frowning over her own book. "You wait here." Old Aunt Yetta took her cane and hobbled out of her house, past the garden, and into the forest, leaving Millie alone with the books.

Millie waited, watching out the window until Old Aunt Yetta was out of sight. Then she climbed onto the counter and balanced on her knees, hoping to raid Old Aunt Yetta's store of ingredients and find brandy and lavender oil and maybe even a snail shell.

There were three shelves full of glass bottles and pouches of various sizes, some with dried leaves or seeds or pods or bark. Then, above the books, above the bottles, on a shelf so high she hadn't been able to see it from the ground, was a row of tiny stoppered glass bottles, each one the size of her thumb, each one labeled in Old Aunt

Yetta's wobbly cursive. Millie plucked a bottle at random and squinted at the label. "For Maximus" it said.

In that instant, crouched on the countertop, among the collected wisdom of generations of Yare, everything came together like a clap of thunder. When Maximus left to do the Mailing, he wore a hat, boots, and gloves—No-Fur clothes, human clothes, the same disguise he wore for Halloweening—but even that was not enough. He'd need to be able to pass as one of them, to go into the posting office to drop off the packages for Etsy and collect whatever the Yare had ordered. He'd need to look like a human. He'd need to lose his fur.

Millie pulled out the cork stopper and sniffed. The liquid had a bracing smell, like peppermint and cloves, that made her eyes water. She wondered how she would look without her fur, what color her skin would be, whether her silvery-gray eyes would look strange to the No-Furs, or whether they'd just think that she was a regular . . .

"Millie?"

Millie froze, clutching the little glass bottle, as she heard the thump of Old Aunt Yetta's cane. "Millie, what are you doing up there?"

Millie tucked the vial into her pocket, knowing that Old Aunt Yetta's eyes were bad.

"Just putting the book away!" she said, and was relieved to hear that her voice sounded normal. She kept her fingers curled around the vial as Old Aunt Yetta puttered around the kitchen, talking to herself, boiling up beetroot and yarrow and cattails from the marsh into a foul-smelling potion that Millie was to swallow every night before bed.

"Don't be forgetting your program tomorrow!" Old Aunt Yetta said as Millie was gathering her things, preparing to leave. "I'll be taping it tonight!"

"Thank you," Millie said, and ran to her friend, throwing her arms around Old Aunt Yetta's waist and hugging her tight.

That night Millie waited until she heard the sounds of her father's deep breaths and her mother's little wheezes. She crept out of her bed, leaving a Millie-shaped pile of pillows beneath the covers. The first two hours of *The Next Stage* were over, but if she swam fast, she'd reach the shore in time for the finale, in time to hear Danna de la Cruz and to see the winner crowned.

At the edge of the water, she pulled the vial out of her pocket, looked at it for a long moment, then tucked it away. She wasn't sure how long the potion would last, so she'd decided not to swallow it until she reached the other side. She stared at the water, gathering her courage. Then she waded out until she couldn't stand, did a shallow dive, and began swimming toward the opposite shore.

She paddled and kicked for what felt like hours . . . but whenever she looked, thinking that she had to be getting there, it didn't seem like she'd gotten any closer to the shore. Her arms got heavy, and her legs got so tired that she could barely move them. She floated on her back, then flipped over, peering for the No-Fur school, but she couldn't see or hear anything, not a single light or a single voice.

Come on, she told herself, and started swimming again . . . but her sodden dress felt like there were stones in its seams, and she was so tired, and her arms were so heavy, and the lake seemed endless. Millie kicked hard, splashing, gasping for air.

She thought of her mother crying after the last time she'd run away, how Septima had sobbed and wrung her hands and said she didn't know what she'd do if anything happened to her Millie, her Little Silver, her Little Bit.

She thought of her father, his grave face as he instructed her not to sing or skip or shout, because the No-Furs would hear, and how sad he'd looked when he'd told her about Demetrius, the brother who'd disappeared.

I don't want to die, Millie thought. She tried to kick harder, but she was so exhausted that her legs barely moved, and she could hardly lift her arms at all before they splashed helplessly down into the lake.

"Help!" she squeaked, thrashing at the water, knowing that no one would hear her. "Help!"

And then, like an answered prayer, there were hands around her shoulders, flipping her onto her back, and a voice saying, "I've got you." Millie let herself float, feeling her body being towed through the water, as strong arms—strong human arms—held her and strong human legs kicked through the water, pulling her to the shore.

CHAPTER 11

Alice

MOST OF HER TIME AT THE CENTER, ALICE had tried to be quiet, to be invisible, to slip, unnoticed, among her classmates. The night after the Jessica Jarvis incident she decided not to care.

Late that night, she stomped up the path to the dining hall, cracking branches, kicking dead leaves, doing everything but banging Phil's bongos to announce her arrival. The dining-hall doors were locked, but instead of looking for the key that she knew Kate kept underneath the mat, Alice slammed the door as hard as she could with her shoulder, giving a humorless smile when it popped open on her first attempt. If they thought she was a monster, well, then, she'd behave like a monster.

Alice yanked open the refrigerator. At the end of that awful, endless day, she'd refused to go to dinner, had stayed in bed, flat on her belly with a pillow over her head.

"Kate made you something special," Lori said after paying a special visit to Bunk Ladybug, but Alice had refused to answer or even move.

Lori hadn't lied. There was a plate in the walk-in refrigerator, covered in wax paper, with "For Alice" written on it in Kate's dashed-off scribble. Last week they'd been experimenting with brownie recipes, adding swirls of dark chocolate, marshmallow drizzle, bits of toffee, and peppermint. It had been fun.

Alice snatched the plate and turned to go. She'd walk to the lake, she'd eat her treat, and then she'd figure out if she even wanted to stay at this place or whether she should just call her parents, admit defeat, and beg them to bring her back home.

On her way out, she stopped and looked at the stack of clean plates on the shelf, the rows of bowls for the morning's porridge, the heavy mugs for tea. Before she'd even planned it, she stretched out her arm and swept a stack of pottery onto the floor. The crash was deafening as the plates and bowls shattered into nasty-looking shards and pottery dust. Alice leaped over the mess, still holding her brownies, and started to walk down to the lake.

The day had been just as horrible as she'd feared. She'd lain awake all night, too ashamed and furious to sleep, and when it was time for Daily Conversation, her eyes felt gritty, like they were full of sand, and her arms and neck were knotted with cramps.

"Oh," she heard Riya say as the girls stepped out of the cabin in the morning. Riya stopped moving like she'd been frozen. Taley gasped.

Alice pushed past them. It looked like the campus had been hit by some strange snowstorm that had left the tree trunks blanketed in white.

Then Alice saw what was going on. Jessica and her crew had had a busy night. It wasn't snow on the trees; it was pieces of paper. Each one of them had her picture. Her picture, with another one beside it. On some posters she was lined up next to a Bigfoot, and sometimes the Thing or the Incredible Hulk or King Kong.

Alice stomped over to a tree and tore down the flyers. She marched to the next tree and saw, out of the corner of her eye, that Riya and Taley were trotting from tree to tree, pulling down more pictures. She'd just finished ripping down a flyer depicting her next to Godzilla when Jessica Jarvis drifted by.

"It really is an uncanny resemblance," Jessica said. She looked lovely as always, her hair in shining waves, the pleats of her miniskirt perfectly ironed, her lip gloss beautifully applied, her white blouse spotless.

Alice's eyes were hot and her throat felt tight and burning as she pulled another poster off a tree. She wanted to ask why . . . but she knew there wasn't an answer that would satisfy her or take away the sting. They'd done this to her because it was what people like Jessica did. It was how they kept themselves on top of the social pyramid . . . every once in a while, they'd step down from their pedestal and squash the people underneath them, just to remind the world that they could.

That morning, classes were canceled. Phil and Lori called everyone to Mother Tree and then stood there in silence, their heads bowed. Lori finally looked up, and Alice was mortified to see that Lori's eyes were full of tears.

"I have never—never—been so disappointed," she said. Her voice was croaky as she slowly looked over the assembled learners. "When you enrolled, each one of you signed a pledge. You promised to respect the individuality and dignity and unique spirit of the other members of this village. This morning, we learned that some of you didn't take that pledge seriously. You have betrayed not only your fellow learners but your own integrity and the spirit in which we founded the Center."

Phil rested his hands on her shoulders as Lori continued. "I urge the person or people who did this—and I hesitate to even dignify you with the title of 'person'—to come forward now, and apologize, not only to Alice, but to this entire community and, maybe most of all, to yourselves."

Lori stepped back. A heavy silence descended over the group. Alice sat, miserable, feeling as if every inch of her skin was burning, as if she could experience her classmates' scorn and pity like a physical thing, a fever or a rash.

After five minutes of silence, Phil said, "My good friend Jack David agreed to come this morning and lead a seminar about bullying. I urge you all to give him your full attention."

Phil bent his head, and a short, bald, sunburned-looking man, dressed in a blue shirt and khakis, bounded to the front of the group and said, "Who here has ever felt like they didn't fit in?"

All morning Alice sat there listening to Jack David talk

about societal standards and internalized self-loathing and "a mind-set of kindness" and how it was all of their duty to stand up to bullies. Lori said the Center would be sending a letter home to everyone's parents "with regard to this unfortunate situation," and Phil once again urged the culprits, or "anyone with any knowledge of the situation," to come forward.

Alice didn't move. *This is what happens,* she told herself. *This is what happens when you're dumb enough to think that anyone actually likes you. This is what happens when you let yourself hope.*

Phil and Lori let her go back to the cabin and spend the entire afternoon there, skipping lunch and her learning sessions and Evening Nutrition. Alice lay on her bed with her eyes closed, ignoring Taley and Riya when they tried to talk to her, ignoring Jessica, who knew better than to say a word.

That night Lori tried to tell her about the brownies Kate had baked, but Alice wouldn't open her eyes. Taley and Riya invited her to watch the finale of some reality TV talent show with them; they'd gotten special permission to use the TV set in the lodge. Alice just shook her head.

"I'mdb sorry thisb habbened," said Taley. She tried to touch Alice's hair.

Alice jerked away.

"Leave. Me. Alone," she said.

"Okay," said Taley. "But we're here if you want to talk or anything." She paused. "We're really sorry." She sounded like she meant it, but Alice thought that she and Riya were privately discussing how they'd warned Alice about Jessica, how they'd told her this would happen, how it was nobody's fault but her own.

Alice lay on her bed, motionless, fists clenched, through lights-out. When everyone was asleep, she got up, slammed out of the cabin, and went to the kitchen, where she took the brownies and broke the dishes. *I don't want to be here,* she thought, stomping off toward the water. *I don't want to be anywhere. I don't want to be . . . at all.*

She'd just gotten herself settled underneath her favorite tree when she heard something. Faint splashing, then a girl's voice.

"Help!"

Alice peered out into the darkness. Maybe she'd imagined something. Maybe this was just another trick, a way for a day she didn't think could get any worse to prove her wrong. She heard more splashing . . . and coughing . . . and a tiny, choking voice saying, "Help!"

Without thinking, she kicked off her shoes and ran into the water, stroking quickly until she reached the flailing figure. *A girl*, she thought, although between the darkness and the churn of the water, it was hard to tell.

"I've got you," she said. Immediately the girl stopped kicking and thrashing, letting Alice grab her shoulders and tow her onto the shore.

CHAPTER 12

Millie

MILLIE FELT HERSELF BEING PULLED THROUGH the water, then dragged up onto the sandy beach. She heard her rescuer collapse beside her, gasping.

As soon as she could move, Millie pushed herself onto her hands and knees, and half crawled, half scuttled into the bushes, so that her savior—a girl, she thought, a No-Fur girl—wouldn't be able to see her. *Never, never, never let a No-Fur catch sight of you*, she'd heard her parents and her teachers and Old Aunt Yetta tell her for years . . . but the tickle of fear was completely overwhelmed by her excitement. She was here, in the No-Fur world. With a No-Fur girl! Her fondest wish had come true.

When she managed to get herself hidden, she retched and opened her mouth, and what felt like half the lake came pouring out. Millie looked down. Her dress was a soaked ruin through which her fur could clearly be seen. Her pockets were empty, the vial of potion lost some-where in the lake's vastness. Her hairy feet, with their curving claws, were bare, which meant her ruby slippers were probably at the bottom of the lake. She patted her head, trying to smooth back her head-hair, and smiled a little as her fingers found the bow she'd clipped in, on the other side of the lake, what felt like a million years ago.

Peeking through the bushes, she saw the other girl get up. She was beautiful, big and solid like Millie always wished she could be, with thick, gleaming hair running down her back, strong, round arms, and tanned legs. The girl deftly twisted her hair into a coil, wringing it out before flipping it over her shoulder and looking around.

"Hello?" she called.

"I am back in here," Millie said. She knew she should just run away, leave before the girl could get a good look at her and tell the grown-ups that she'd just fished a real, live Bigfoot out of the lake, but Millie couldn't make her-self do it. How many times had she dreamed of a night like this, where she'd meet one of the No-Fur kids and

they'd talk and discover all the things they had in common and become friends? All thoughts of the *Next Stage*
finale had fled in the presence of a real, live No-Fur girl.
Millie had a million questions, and this could be the only
chance she'd have in her entire life to get answers.

"Are you okay?" the No-Fur girl was asking. Now she'd
taken off her top-shirt and was repeating the wringing-
out process. Millie could see muscles flex in her back as
her hands worked, and felt her familiar shame at being so
puny. And how would she explain why she was standing
in the bushes?

She did some fake coughing to buy herself some time
and decided to trust the girl with at least a small piece of
the truth. "I am okay," she said. "It is only that my dress is
kind of see-through, and I am a little bit . . . hairy."

The girl winced—a sympathetic kind of wince,
Millie thought.

"Is your stomach okay?" she asked. "Do you need a
drink?"

"That would be lovely!" Millie said in a fancy kind
of voice like the one she'd heard in a commercial for a
luxurious brand of mustard. "Also maybe a small snackle?
That was a very long swim."

The No-Fur girl looked puzzled. Millie worried that

maybe she'd been rude or said something wrong. "I have brownies," the girl finally said. Sure enough, the girl looked around, then walked up the beach a ways and came back with a plate.

Brownies! Millie had seen commercials for them but had never tasted one. Before she could stop herself, her hand shot through the bushes and snatched a dark-brown square of pastry from the top of the plate. "Thank you," she said, and took a tiny nibble. The rich, dense sweetness seemed to explode on her tongue, filling her mouth and throat with unimaginable deliciousness. Millie moaned out loud.

"I know," said the No-Fur, sounding shy and proud. "I came up with the recipe by myself."

Millie crammed a bite of brownie into her mouth and closed her eyes, chewing in ecstasy. If No-Furs had these, if they could eat them anytime they wanted, how did they ever get anything done? Why would they want to do anything else? If Millie was a No-Fur, she'd just eat brownies all day and all night.

Except now she was thirsty.

"Excuse me, but did you perhaps mention water?" she asked, taking care to keep her language polite and correct.

"I'll go get some," said the girl. She turned on her heel and started to run toward the school.

Leave, said a voice in Millie's head, a voice that sounded like Septima's. *Leave now and this could come round right.* Instead, Millie helped herself to another two brownies. The girl couldn't see her through the bushes—at least, not that well—and even if she did, Millie would use the line that all Yare littlies had been taught to say as soon as they could speak, the line they were instructed to recite if ever the No-Furs found them: *I have a glandular condition.*

She shook her fur briskly, sending drops of water splashing onto the shrubbery and the sand, and gobbled the first brownie, then ate the second one in tiny little nibbles to make it last. She was considering whether she could put a few in her pockets when the girl came back. The No-Fur girl was holding a glass bottle of water and another bottle of milk and had a stack of towels and a dark-blue sweater with a hood tucked under her arm.

"Here," she said, passing the bottles and the towels and clothing through the bushes. "These are from the lost-and-found."

Millie didn't know what a lost-and-found was. She drank half the water, then struggled to pull the sweater over her head, briefly getting tangled in the hood. The sweater smelled sweet and felt soft and had a pocket in front for her hands.

"Thank you," she said. "I am Millie. And who might you be?"

"I'm Alice," said the No-Fur.

"Alice," Millie repeated, tasting the name. *Alice and Millie*. They sounded good together.

"Are you sure you're okay? Do you want to see the nurse? Or take a shower?" Alice asked. "We can go back to my cabin."

"Nyebbeh!" Millie almost shouted. At Alice's silence, she remembered her grand-sounding voice. "I mean, 'No, thank you.'" Of course, she would have loved to explore the school and to take a shower—the Yare only had tubs—and see what other No-Fur goods she could acquire from the found-and-lost, but she knew she couldn't risk exposing herself to more than one No-Fur at a time.

She lowered her voice. "No, I'll be a-okay. It's warm enough out. I'll be drying soon." She tightened the strings of the hood. "This sweating-shirt is nice and warm."

"Sweatshirt," said Alice, who sounded amused.

"Sweatshirt," Millie repeated, and filed the word away. "So, Alice, do you live in this school?"

"Yep." Millie wasn't sure, but she didn't think that

Alice sounded entirely happy about it. "I've been here since September."

"And where is your home?"

"New York City."

Millie couldn't keep herself from bouncing on the balls of her feet with glee. New York City was where the *Friends* lived, where movie stars and other famous people lived, and where *The Next Stage* was filmed. She had wanted to know everything about New York—about the subway and whether Alice lived in a skyscraper and if she knew any movie stars and if she had ever seen the Thanksgiving Day Parade—but before she could begin, the No-Fur asked some questions of her own.

"Were you trying to swim the whole way across the lake? Where did you come from?"

Oh, dear. Millie coughed for a while, trying to come up with a story.

"I was camping with my parents, Ross and Rachel," she began. "On the other side of the lake. In a tent. With a lantern and the bags-of-sleep."

"Sleeping bags?" asked Alice.

Millie paused. "As you said. But then Ross's pet monkey, Marcel, ran into the lake! I was chasing Marcel, and he was swimming away, and then I was all the way in the middle of the water, and then I was here." Millie paused, praying that Alice was buying this. "Did you happen to have seen a small monkey?"

"No, I haven't seen a monkey. Your parents are going to freak out if they wake up and see that you aren't there."

Freak out. What did that mean? "Yes," Millie ventured. "But they are very good sleepers." She sighed. "I should go back, though. Just as soon as I catch onto my breath." But she couldn't leave until she'd asked at least a few of her questions. "How many are here? Do you miss your parents? Do you ever go home? Do you take a train or a plane? Are you having any brothers or sisters or pets? What is your favorite show on TV?"

Alice was laughing. "Slow down! One question at a time!"

"All right, yes," Millie agreed.

"Where do you go to school?" Alice asked.

Millie had an answer for this. "I am homeschooled," she said. "With a few other kids in my village."

Alice seemed to accept that. "And where do you live? When you're not camping?"

"Oh, not far," said Millie, gesturing vaguely toward the other side of the lake.

Then, before Alice could ask her more questions that she wouldn't be able to answer, Millie blurted, "Do you have a favorite singer? Have you ever been to a concert? Do you know how to do ice-skating? Can you ride a bike?"

"Let's see," Alice said, lifting her fingers with each answer. "I can ice-skate and ride a bike, but I don't ever really ride my bike except in the summertime on Cape Cod. My favorite TV show is *Gilmore Girls*—I watched two whole seasons this summer with my granny—and I take my parents' car home."

"You can drive?" Millie gasped.

"Oh, no. They have a driver. He comes. Let's see . . . I don't have any brothers or sisters or pets. My father's allergic."

"To children or animals?" asked Millie.

Alice laughed, and Millie did too, wondering why the other girl hadn't answered the question about whether she missed her parents, and also what kind of parents would send a littlie away.

Alice sat on a patch of grass next to the bushes and flipped her thick, beautiful hair over her shoulders. Millie sighed. "It must be nice to live with lots of other girls. I bet you are having many friends."

167

"No," Alice said briefly. With that one word her whole expression changed. She wilted, like the flowers after Florrie dumped a whole can of water on them instead of just sprinkling it gently. Her chin tucked into her chest and her eyes turned toward the ground.

"Why not?" Millie asked.

"Because I look funny," said Alice.

"What do you mean?"

Alice frowned and paused. Millie wondered if she'd done something wrong or asked a rude question.

"Because of my hair," Alice finally said, touching her curls. "Because of my feet," she said, arranging herself so that she was sitting on them before Millie could get a good look. Then, with her head bowed and her chin almost touching her chest, she muttered, "Because I'm ugly, and I'm so much bigger than the rest of them."

Millie was shocked. "You are not ugly!" Millie said. "You are beautiful!"

Alice was half smiling and shaking her head.

"You saved my life! You're lucky to be so big and strong. In my Tribe . . ." Millie bit her lip, hoping Alice hadn't heard, then started again. "In my village, being big is good fortune. It means you're strong and fast." She sighed. "I wish . . ." But never mind what she wished. She wanted to learn everything she could about Alice. "Do you get to go to movies?"

"Sometimes," Alice said. "There's a theater in Standish."

"Have you ever been on a plane?"

"Yes, lots of times."

"And when are you seeing your parents?"

"On vacations," Alice said. "Every few months, and then in the summertime."

"Every few months." Millie couldn't believe it. She hardly went even a few minutes without seeing her parents. "They must be missing you oh so much."

"I don't think my parents miss me much at all," Alice said. "They send me away all the time. Schools, camps..."

Millie's eyes got wide. "Since you were a littlie?"

Alice nodded. "I'm only really with them a few weeks out of the year."

"So you do as you please." Millie felt jealousy like a worm twisting in her tummy. "My parents don't leave me alone, not ever. When I'm in the garden, or swimming or in the kitchen, they are there. Once"—she dropped her voice—"my mother followed me to lessons. We were doing spelling and I looked out the window and saw her feet behind the mulberry bush."

"One time, my mother left me at the Metropolitan

Museum of Art," Alice countered. "I was in kinder-garten and we were on a school trip and the parents were supposed to pick us up at the museum instead of our school, only my mother forgot. She didn't even send a nanny."

"My mother," said Millie, "used to chew my food for me when I was little. She said I had tiny teeth and was needing her help."

"My mother made me order my school uniforms for kindergarten by myself," Alice said. "She gave me a catalog and a credit card and told me to buy whatever I needed."

"My mother makes me dresses that match hers," said Millie.

"I'm too big to wear my mother's dresses," Alice said in a voice so quiet that Millie wasn't sure she was meant to hear it. She wondered exactly how small Alice's mother was, and if she had some illness or disease that kept her child-size.

"So your parents are pretty strict?" Alice asked.

"You have none of the idea!" Millie said. Her fur was now dry and bristling with indignation, and she must have sounded funny, because Alice was smiling. "They are not letting me watch shows of my choosing. They shush me when I sing. They make me work in the garden and tend the goat, and when I grow up I'll have to take over my father's job"—she stuttered briefly over the word "job"—"and I won't get to pick my own way."

"What's your father's job?" Alice asked.

Thinking fast, Millie came up with a true-ish kind of answer. "He has a farm," she said.

"So you'll be a farmer?"

Close enough, thought Millie. "I'll be the boss of a farm."

"And . . . you don't want to be on a farm?"

"I want to sing," said Millie with such forcefulness that she was surprised the tree branches didn't shake and shed their leaves. "I want to be famous and on TV, and I could, I think, I could maybe do it if they would only let me try, but they won't. They don't even want me to be watching *The Next Stage*, and it is my very favorite!"

Alice considered this. "Can't you watch it somewhere else? At a friend's house or something?"

"There is only one TV set in my village."

Alice looked shocked. "Only one TV? Are you, like, Amish?" she asked.

Millie held her breath. Was "Amish" another No-Fur word for "Bigfoot"? But, no . . . Alice had asked it way too casually, as if "Amish" was something exotic, but not strange and dangerous and possibly not even real, like a Bigfoot.

"Not Amish," Millie said. "They just don't believe that television is improving."

She exhaled in relief when Alice nodded, feeling like she'd vaulted over a high, invisible hurdle.

"We have one TV set here, in the lodge," said Alice. "They mostly show us educational movies, about Egypt and things like that. But I bet I could get permission to watch something else." She paused and made a face that Millie couldn't read. "They owe me."

"Why?" she asked. "Why are they owing you?"

"Something happened," said Alice. Her tone warned Millie not to push. Millie could have told Alice that the show's season was over, that there wouldn't be new shows until the spring, but then she wouldn't have an excuse to come back, and she already knew that she wanted to come back, to spend more time in this girl's company and learn more about the world that had fascinated her for so long.

"Will you still be camping next week?" Alice asked.

"Yes!" Millie said. "My parents have taken me out of school for a . . . sem-ester." She pronounced the word with care and hoped it was the right one.

"They can leave their farm for that long?" Alice asked.

"Oh, well, the farm is near the camping. We are in a community with others. Phoebe and Monica and Joey and Chandler," said Millie. "They can help with the chores while we are away. If I could sneak away . . . I could meet you. . . ."

"We could watch together. I could make popcorn. . . ." Alice suddenly got quiet. "I mean, if you want me to watch with you."

"Of course I do!" said Millie, who still couldn't believe her good fortune. She paused. "Will there be other No . . ." She snapped her mouth shut before she could say "Furs." "Other kids there?"

Through the bushes, Millie could see that Alice had a strange, unhappy expression on her face.

"It is only that other kids sometimes think I am strange," Millie explained.

Alice brightened. "Me too," she said. "They think I'm strange too."

This made no sense. If Alice lived in Millie's Tribe, she'd be the best-loved girl, more popular, even, than Tulip. *No-Furs must be strange not to appreciate her,* Millie thought. She certainly wouldn't make the same mistake. This No-Fur named Alice had saved her life.

She also had access to a television set and she'd given Millie brownies and . . .

Millie looked up at the sky, which was just starting to shift from black to gray. She imagined her mother waking up and finding pillows, instead of Millie, in her bed.

"I should go," she said.

"Do you have a phone?" Alice asked. "So I can text you?"

"No," said Millie, "but I'm on-the-line. I have an email address." This was a secret that not even Old Aunt Yetta knew. The year before, Millie had set up an account so that she could vote for her favorites on *The Next Stage.* She paused, then shyly recited, "FurryMillie@standishonline.com."

"I think I can remember that," said Alice. "I'll write to you."

"I'll write back!" Millie trotted down the path, hoping that in the dark her new friend wouldn't notice her fur, and feeling happier than she had in a long time. "So long! Farewell!" she called.

When she turned to look back, Alice was standing there, waving and watching her go.

CHAPTER 13

Alice

OVER THE NEXT WEEK MILLIE AND ALICE MET twice, at midnight, on the shores of Lake Standish. As soon as she was sure her roommates were asleep, Alice would slip out of bed. She would take a snack and a glass bottle of milk from the dining-hall kitchen and would wait on the shore for Millie to arrive.

Her new friend was odd, Alice thought, watching Millie paddle to the shore in her canoe. She would only come over on moonless nights, explaining that her village adhered to the lunar calendar, and that it was bad luck to travel on nights when the moon was out. She wore oversize sweatpants that drooped past her ankles, a big plaid shirt with sleeves that came practically to her fingertips, and a baseball cap pulled down low on her forehead. The second time she'd come, she'd hopped out of her canoe and dashed behind the bushes—to pee, Alice thought—except then she'd stayed there. Alice had been trying to figure out a polite way to ask why she was hiding when, from her spot behind the foliage, Millie had explained that she had a glandular condition that caused her to have hair on her face and hands, "And I am shy of being seen."

"Can't you get laser treatments?"

Millie paused. "My parents don't believe in them," she said. That made sense, because, Alice had learned, Millie belonged to a very strict religious order. Its practitioners, who called themselves the Yare, had rules that prohibited movies, music, and any television show except for *Friends* and *The Next Stage*, which Alice thought was weird, but maybe no weirder than religions that let their followers drink everything but coffee or required them to wear little hats or didn't celebrate birthdays.

Millie had been homeschooled and had lived her whole life in a Yare village that was somewhere upstate, she'd said, gesturing vaguely across the water. "Not too far from here." The Yare were mostly farmers, although some of the women did knitting and crochet and needlework that they sold "on-the-line," which was how Millie referred to the Internet. Millie had hardly ever been out of her village, had never met a kid who wasn't Yare, and had about eighteen million questions every time she saw Alice. That night, after they'd shared the homemade granola bars and apple pie that Alice had made with Kate that afternoon and filched from the kitchen, they were discussing what they'd started to call "the *Friends* exception."

"I mean, it sounds like a funny show, but I don't understand why the . . . Elders?" Alice looked at Millie, who nodded—or at least it looked like she was nodding through the bushes. "Why the Elders would think it was any better than, like, *Gilmore Girls* or *Modern Family*."

"I cannot speak for them," said Millie, and then gave a little giggle. "Oh, they'd laugh if they heard me saying that. I am always speaking. About everything. Old Aunt Yetta calls me a box of chatter." She took a deep breath. Alice braced herself for the onslaught of questions that she knew was coming.

"Have you ever been to a restaurant?" Millie asked.

"Ever?" asked Alice.

"I mean to say, which restaurant is your favorite one?" Millie said quickly.

Alice told her about the candy store in Cape Cod

that served cheddar-cheese-and-chive scones and dark-chocolate-covered apricots.

"Apricots," Millie said dreamily. "I'll have to ask my papa to order me some. What is your favorite place that you've ever been?"

Alice smiled. "The beach with my granny," she said. "In the mornings, when there's no one there, I go running on the sand. Sometimes at low tide there are sandbars—little islands," she explained, and told Millie how she'd wade through the shallows to reach them, and then pretend that she'd been shipwrecked and would have to survive, all alone.

"You like to be alone?" Millie asked.

Alice didn't want to answer that. She didn't want to tell Millie the truth about how lonely she was and how she longed for company, only nobody ever seemed to want to be around her. "My turn," she said instead. After their first meeting, they'd agreed that for every ten questions Millie asked, Alice could ask two. "What's the name of your town? Is it far from here?"

"Not so far," said Millie. "But you must not try and find it!"

"Why not?" Alice asked.

"The Elders—my parents especially—they don't like

us talking with the N— I mean, with the outsiders," Millie said. "They wouldn't like it if they knew I had made up a friend."

"Made a friend," Alice said. She liked the funny way Millie said things. "If you say 'made up,' it sounds like I'm imaginary."

"Ah," said Millie. "Also, we don't like people to look at us."

"Because of the . . ." Instead of saying the word "hair," Alice merely gestured toward her face. Millie had explained that lots of the Yare shared her affliction and didn't like going out in public.

"Exactly," said Millie. "So are you having a best friend? At home, in New York?"

Alice looked down at her feet. She felt sick and ashamed as she heard Millie scoot closer.

"Did I ask something wrong?" Millie asked in a small voice.

Alice shook her head. "It's not your fault," she said. "I don't really . . ." She took a deep breath. "People don't like me," she finally said.

"I like you," said Millie.

Alice gave an unhappy laugh. "You don't know many other girls."

"Even if I knew one hundred girls, you would be my bestie," Millie said.

Alice found that she was on the verge of tears. "Well, you don't go to school here," she said. "None of the girls here are my friends."

"What do they do?"

Alice paused . . . and then, without knowing she was going to say anything, she blurted, "They took my picture."

"What?" Millie asked. "Who took your picture?"

"Some of the kids here. They tricked me into skinny-dipping." Alice gave an unhappy bark of laughter. "Or fat-dipping, I guess you'd call it, in my case."

"I don't know what that is," said Millie.

"It's when you swim naked," said Alice. "So, when I was in the water, they stole all my clothes, and when I came out, they took my picture, and they put it up, all over campus." She sniffled and swiped at her cheeks. "For all I know, they even put it online for everyone to laugh at it."

"Oh, Alice," Millie said. "Oh no!"

"And it's not the other girls," said Alice. She was glad for the darkness, glad that she was probably just a girl-shaped lump on the shore. Tears were slipping down her face, soaking the collar of her sweatshirt as she voiced her deepest fear. "It's me."

"What do you mean? What about you?" asked Millie.

"Everywhere I go, every single school, the same thing happens. Nobody likes me. Nobody ever likes me! My roommates here are only nice because they have to be. My own parents . . ." Alice's voice caught. "My own parents don't even like me. They keep sending me away."

"I like you," said Millie. Her voice was firm. She got to her feet, emerged from the bushes, and wrapped her arms around Alice's shoulders, hugging her from behind. "Who did that?" Millie asked. "Who stole your clothes and took your picture? Who did that to you?"

Alice's voice hitched and wobbled. "It doesn't matter," she said. "It doesn't matter which one, because if it wasn't that girl, it would have been someone else. It's me," she said, and now there was no way that Millie wouldn't hear her crying. "There's something wrong with me."

"There is nothing wrong with you," Millie said, and rested her chin on the top of Alice's head. "Probably they are jealous of your beauty."

Alice gave a bitter little snort and wondered if Millie, too, was teasing her. Millie pressed on.

"I'd give anything to look like you. If I was bigger, I could be keeping up, and the other Yare wouldn't ditch me," she said. "If I was stronger and faster, they wouldn't treat me like I'm a little scrap of nothing. If my fu—if my hair wasn't so strange . . ."

"My hair is strange," said Alice.

"Your hair is perfect." Millie released Alice and plopped down beside her, straightening the baseball cap that covered her head and shadowed her face. "If you lived in my village, you would be the most favorite of all, I promise. Even Tulip couldn't compete."

Alice laughed . . . only now she felt lighter inside, now that she'd shared the story of what had happened. When Millie leaned against her, Alice didn't pull away. The two girls sat, shoulder to shoulder, talking and laughing until the sky lightened from black to gray and it was time for Millie to paddle back home.

CHAPTER 14

Jeremy

Some boys rode their bikes home from school or walked to soccer or football practice or went into Standish's two-block-long downtown to buy cheeseburgers and ice-cream cones and hang out at the library. Jeremy had a different routine.

As soon as the last bell rang, he gathered up his books and hurried home, keeping his eyes open on the path through the woods, looking for bent twigs and broken branches and any sign of a Bigfoot nearby. Sometimes, while he walked, he imagined himself in front of a cheering crowd, explaining how he'd found and captured a Bigfoot. Sometimes he envisioned a TV interview, the suit and tie he'd be wearing when Donnetta Dale, lead anchor from Channel 6 Eyewitness News, leaned intently toward him, asking, "How were you able to remain so committed to your quest, even in the face of relentless scorn and disbelief?"

On that fateful Thursday, he hooked his finger into the handle of a quart of milk, dumped a box of cereal into a mixing bowl, and poured the milk on top. While he ate, he made the rounds of his favorite websites: Paranormal Activity, Area 51, Weird Roswell, and AliensAmongUs. The last website was his favorite—it was where Bigfoot hunters posted rumors and, occasionally, pictures that claimed to show actual Bigfoots.

There hadn't been anything new on the site in weeks, though. Jeremy didn't feel optimistic as he clicked over and saw . . . nothing but a blank screen. He refreshed his browser and stared at the message that showed a frowny-face emoji and the words *We have crashed under heavy traffic. Please keep trying!* He hit refresh over and over, spooning cereal into his mouth with his eyes on the screen, telling himself not to get his hopes up, even as one of his feet started tapping in a jittery rhythm on the floor.

It wasn't nothing. When the site finally let him in, he saw a picture of a flyer with two photographs side by side. Jeremy's heart jumped into his throat as he recognized the shot on the left, a picture with which he was intimately familiar, a female Bigfoot in profile, caught in midstride, the still from the Patterson-Gimlin film that he'd used in his report.

The picture on the right was what made his mouth go dry and his skin prickle. It was a photograph of a smaller person in the same sideways pose, hunched over, one arm slung across her chest, her body bristling with . . . Jeremy squinted, holding his breath, staring at the low-resolution image, trying to believe what he was seeing.

Fur. Pine needles and mud too—maybe just pine needles and mud, Jeremy cautioned himself. He couldn't see the figure's feet clearly, but it was big, big and broad-shouldered, with large hands and wild, bushy hair. More than its size and posture, though, was the attitude of shame and fear communicated in the slump of its shoulders, the curve of its neck, the way it tried to hide its face and body.

"Oh my God," Jeremy whispered. His face was flushed; his heart was hammering so hard he was surprised his mother, in her office down the hall, hadn't heard it.

Separated at birth? read the words underneath the pictures . . . and that was all it said. There were no names, of course, no location, no clue as to where the shot had been taken (and, his brain whispered, it could have been a fake, was probably a fake, Photoshopped and whomped up on someone's computer as a joke).

Except his heart told him otherwise. In his two years of seeking, of research, he'd seen, he reckoned, every fake Bigfoot picture that existed online, and he'd never seen this one. He'd never seen anything that looked like this, that communicated the same kind of painful, aching fear.

"Real," he whispered, then read the site's caption out loud. "We have no information where this image, posted anonymously online, came from," read the text. "All we know for sure is that the computer's IP address is associated with a server in upstate New York."

"Real," he said again.

"Talking to yourself?" asked Noah, who'd come up from his basement hideaway. Jeremy ignored him. He slammed his laptop shut, shoved it in his backpack, and speed-dialed the first contact on his phone with one hand as he carried his empty mixing bowl to the kitchen.

"Did you see it?" Jo's familiar voice asked.

"Saw it," Jeremy answered. "I'm on my way." He'd almost made it to the door when his mother drifted out of her office. A pencil anchored her bun to her head, and her eyes looked dreamy.

"Jeremy?" she said. "Where are you going?"

"Cub Scouts," he answered.

Suzanne frowned. "Are you still a Cub Scout?"

Jeremy had actually never been a Cub Scout. "Absolutely," he said. "I'll be back late!" He ran out the door, jumped on his bike, and pedaled down the street toward Jo's house as fast as he could. Her street, normally empty, was unusually crowded. A van that read "Standish Plumbers—DUMP IT ON US" was parked at the curb, next to a gray sedan and a motorcycle. Jeremy dropped his bike on her lawn and went inside without knocking, knowing that the door would be unlocked and that Jo would be in her chair on the sunporch. She'd already pulled up the flyer on the biggest of her four computer screens and was doing a point-by-point comparison between the two images.

"Do we know where it's from?" Jeremy said as he tried to look over Jo's shoulder while catching his breath. "All the site said was upstate New York."

"The picture was uploaded on an iPhone with a New York City area code," Jo said without turning away from the screen.

"How do you know that?" Sometimes, the things that Jo did, or found out, did not strike him as entirely legal.

She tweaked her ponytail, leaning closer to the screen.

"I have my ways. I already forwarded it to Gary."

Gary Hardison was an online friend of Jo's, a PhD student in California just as obsessed with Bigfoots as they were.

"He should be able to compare the anatomy. He'll tell us if this is the real deal or just a kid in a costume. Our job," she said, spinning her chair so that she faced Jeremy, "is to figure out who posted this picture, and from where."

"So how do we do that? Do we call every single cell phone with a New York City area code and say, 'Did you happen to photograph a Bigfoot in upstate New York recently?'"

Jeremy figured that Jo had a better plan . . . and he wasn't wrong.

"I've been in the Google cache for hours. The image was first uploaded to Blabber. It's one of those apps where kids in high school and college can post things about their professors or other kids. It's all 'supposed to be' anonymous," Jo said, her tone turning sarcastic, her fingers curving into the air quotes she'd put around "supposed to be." Jo could be sharp-tongued, and she saved most of her scorn for people who didn't understand the Internet the way she did—a group that included the vast majority of humanity, as well as Jeremy himself.

"It's also supposed to automatically delete after sixty seconds, but you know how that goes."

Jeremy nodded, and he and Jo recited together, "On the Internet, everything lives forever."

"So anyhow," Jo continued, "all we have to do now is find the Blabber account that posted it."

"How are we going to do that?"

Jo just smiled. Jeremy wondered, maybe for the hundredth time, whether Jo knew people in the government, or whether her father, who he'd heard moving around in the house but had never seen, was some kind of spy.

"Leave that part to me. Meanwhile, your job is to monitor the Net. Especially anything coming from this region."

"The picture was uploaded from somewhere in upstate," Jeremy said, thinking out loud. "That could be here or Albany or up near Vermont . . ."

Jo was unperturbed. "We have to start somewhere, so why not close to home? We know there are Bigfoots in Standish. We know that Standish is in upstate New York. Thus, it's not impossible, and maybe even likely, that the picture was shot somewhere nearby." She smiled her sarcastic half smile. "And sometimes you get lucky. Or so I've heard."

Jeremy wondered what that meant. When Jo turned back to her screen, he started mentally listing the chat rooms he'd hang out in, the Twitter accounts he'd check, the blogs he'd be visiting. "Maybe I'll walk around the forest a little," he said. "If there's a tribe somewhere nearby, like we think, they must be freaking out if they know one of them's been photographed."

"Excellent." Jo's voice was crisp, and Jeremy felt his face flush with pleasure. "As soon as I hear from Gary about what we're looking at, I'll let you know."

Together, they spent the next hour in the Batcave, with Jo scrolling through phone numbers, cross-referencing them with Blabber accounts, and Jeremy googling for other re-postings of, and comments beneath, the flyer. When Jo's father called her to dinner, Jeremy told her good-bye and walked toward his bike, thinking he'd go the long way home through the forest, when his cell phone rang. *Blocked number,* read the screen. Curious, he lifted the phone to his ear. "Hello?"

"Jeremy." The voice was an old man's, cracked and whispery but somehow still powerful, like it belonged to someone who was used to having people listen and do what he said. "Keep looking."

"Keep looking for what?" His heart was beating hard,

and the cereal was sloshing uncomfortably in his belly. "Keep looking where?"

"The forest," said the voice. "The lake. Pay attention to the school. You're very close, boy. Closer than you know."

"Who is this?" He realized—later than he should have—that he and Jo weren't the only people who'd seen the flyer, not if it was floating around online. "And if this is about . . . you know, Bigfoots . . . you should talk to Jo, too."

The man made a rude, dismissive noise. "Never mind the girl," he said. "She'll just slow you down. Keep looking." His voice sounded scary and greedy when he whispered, "We're almost there."

"What do you mean?" Jeremy blurted. "Why do you care?"

"Because they're everything," the old man whispered. "The key to everything." The line went dead. Jeremy stared at the phone, then picked up his bike and gave a shocked yell when it fell to pieces in his hands, as if every bolt had been unscrewed precisely to the point of it coming undone. The wheels went rolling off in opposite directions, the seat and seat post and frame fell to the ground, and Jeremy was left standing there holding the handlebars, hearing that ancient, scratchy, greedy voice in his head, saying, *Because they're everything.*

CHAPTER 15

Millie

"MILLIE?" SEPTIMA STOOD IN THE DOORWAY of Millie's bedroom, her hands entwined, fingers tugging at her wrist-fur. "You barely had two bites at the feast."

"I'm not hungry." Millie was lying on her bed, fully clothed, face toward the wall. It was Halloween, Halloween night, except Halloweening had been canceled after Old Aunt Yetta came across a new picture that had been posted on-the-line, a shot "that proves, conclusively, once and for all, that Bigfoots are real!"

Millie hadn't seen the picture. Hidden in the Lookout Tree, watching the Elders' meeting, she was too far away to get a good look at what it showed. From what she could hear, though, it sounded like the Yare, or at least Old Aunt Yetta, didn't believe that it was real.

"Not Yare. It's the old picture of Cassoundra, and then just a No-Fur littlie with some pine needles and some mud," Old Aunt Yetta pronounced. Millie felt her fur prickle and bristle with alarm. Could that be the picture Alice had told her about, the flyers the mean girls had posted showing her alongside an assortment of monsters?

Nugget, she thought. *I should say something.* Instead, she just listened.

Ricardan glared fiercely at Old Aunt Yetta. "Real or not doesn't matter! If the No-Furs believe it, they'll come looking, and it won't be long before they find us."

"We should go," whispered Aelia, who'd been tugging so hard at the fur on her cheeks that she'd given herself a few bald patches. "We should pack up the village . . . we should go somewhere far . . . where there aren't any cities . . . maybe up north, where it's cold . . ."

"We can't leave," said Junie, one of the younger female Yare. "I just planted my perennials."

"And why would the No-Furs look here?" Old Aunt Yetta asked. "None of them are knowing where the picture was taken. There's nothing that would draw them to our forest."

"Measures must be taken," Ricardan said as his wife nodded her enthusiastic agreement. "Always safe. Never sorry. We must have new rules about noise. Perhaps guards at the perimeter. And we should cancel Halloweening."

At this a chorus of gasps came from some of the younger Yare.

"No Halloweening?" whispered Frederee, whose fur seemed to droop.

"Silence! You don't have the Speaking Stick," Ricardan said, lip curled disdainfully to show his large front teeth. "Halloweening was always foolishness. Far too risky. We can be having our own feasting, and that will be that."

Millie gave a soft growl, feeling like she'd cry. She knew what a Yare celebration would include: rabbit casserole and sweet stewed pumpkin, sweet and savory hand-pies, baked apples and poached pears and sugar-roasted walnuts. Games of checkers and chess and Scrabble played quietly around the fire. No dashing down strange streets, right along with the No-Fur kids, no walking up to No-Fur doorsteps bold as could be, ringing their doorbells, holding your bag open, waiting for them to drop delicious chocolate candy inside. No shouts and no laughter. No pretending, the way Millie always did, that she was a No-Fur girl in a Bigfoot costume, that, at the end of the night, she'd pull off fur-covered boots, unpeel her sleeves and cuffs and wig, and unzip her skin, stepping out of it and leaving it puddled on the floor, to emerge a smooth-skinned little girl, no different from the fairies and princesses and witches and superheroes with whom she'd spent the night.

"They don't know where to look," Old Aunt Yetta snapped.

"They'll find us." Aelia's voice was almost a moan. "They'll be coming . . . with their hellercopters . . . and their bright lights . . . and their littlies on the ATM machines . . ."

"ATVs," whispered Millie, and rolled her eyes.

"Silence," she heard her father rumble. "Ricardan is right." Ricardan preened, his fur bristling, making him look bushier and bigger. "It's too risky. There will be no Halloweening this year."

Millie had almost jumped out of the tree in frustration and fury. Instead she decided, that minute, that she would have her Halloweening, that she'd go trick-or-treating no matter what her father decreed.

By then she'd crossed the lake three times already to visit with Alice. Each time she'd borrowed Frederee's clothing, although she supposed it wasn't technically borrowing because she hadn't technically asked for permission to wear his clothes or to take the Tribe's single canoe. She had eaten brownies and cookies and granola, and had listened as Alice had wept about how much being called a monster and a freak had hurt her, and offered what comfort she could.

Now that Millie had met an actual No-Fur, she could see that maybe No-Fur life wasn't as grand as she'd imagined and that being Yare was maybe not so bad at all. Yare mothers and fathers did not abandon their littlies, putting their lives in the hands of educational consultants, sending them away to sleepaway camps and boarding schools, seeing them only a handful of days every year. If Alice had been Yare, she would have been treasured.

While the grown-up Yare were still chanting their final blessings, Millie had slipped out of the tree, raced to Old Aunt Yetta's house, and pulled the top-lap out from its box underneath Old Aunt Yetta's bed. She logged on to the email account she'd created and sent a message to Alice that read, "Can I go trick-or-treating with you?"

Then she sat, fidgeting and looking over her shoulder, until finally she had her answer: "Yes!!!"

The night of Halloween, Millie, who'd been in what her mother called "a mood" since the decision was made, had left the feasting early and spent the night in bed. At seven o'clock she announced that she was going for a walk.

"By yourself?" Septima asked. She kept her voice gentle, but her hands were working, plucking at her apron or the fur on her fingers.

"I want to be alone," said Millie, taking care to sound extra pouty. "But I would like a small snackle." Her mother filled her packsack with treats from the feasting, and Millie walked down to the lake, glad it was a cloudy night. The canoe was right where she'd left it the last time. It was the work of just a few minutes to slide the boat into the water and start paddling toward the opposite shore.

Alice was waiting for her, dressed in a long coat with a belt, a banded hat, and a pair of dark sunglasses that were pushed up on her forehead so she could see. "Millie! You're here!" she said, and smiled and gave Millie a hug before looking her over, seeing Millie as she really was, in all her furred glory, for the first time. "Wow." Millie had fashioned a kind of hood with a collar out of a piece of brown velvet from Septima's scrap bag. She wore Florrie's work boots and carried one of Old Aunt Yetta's walking sticks.

"Are you an Ewok?" Alice asked.

"An Ewok," Millie confirmed. The No-Furs usually guessed "Bigfoot" when they saw the larger littlies trick-or-treating. When they saw Millie, they typically said

"Ewok," which, Millie had learned on-the-line, were the small, teddy bear–ish creatures that lived on a made-up moon called Endor and whose presence had ruined a movie called *Return of the Jedi*. Millie smoothed her fur as Alice circled her.

"Wow," she said. "That is some costume."

"The Yare are excellent seamstresses," Millie said. This was true—at least, according to the customers who'd posted reviews on Etsy.

"Come on," Alice said. "We're going to trick-or-treat on campus first, and then they're taking us into town."

Millie marched up the hill, following her friend, who adjusted her pace so that Millie didn't have to struggle to keep up. The air was crisp, and smelled like autumn, like fallen leaves and fireplaces, and Millie couldn't stop looking at the No-Fur kids in their costumes. Some were dressed as superheroes, with boots and capes and papier-mâché shields. There was a boy whose hair looked like it had been electrified, with his face painted white and his lips painted black, and a girl in an enormous white hoop-skirted gown and a matching white hat with a green satin brim. From the way Alice avoided her, Millie guessed that this was the infamous Jessica, who'd tricked Alice into thinny-dipping and taken her picture.

"I should warn you," Alice said. "The stuff the learning guides hand out is probably going to be, like, no-bake kale cookies or something."

Millie nodded. She didn't care about the candy and had her small snackle and a thermos of tea in case she got hungry. She looked at her friend. "And what are you being?"

Alice sighed, pulling her hat down tightly over her forehead. "I'm the Invisible Man."

Millie, assuming this was another reference to a book she hadn't read or a TV show she'd never seen, simply nodded. After hearing what had happened to Alice, she understood why her friend would want to be invisible.

"Hi, Alice!" said a girl dressed all in white, with a white helmet and face mask, who was carrying a slim, silver sword.

"Who's your friendb?" snuffled a girl in a fancy, flounced green dress, with a green wig and green face paint.

"This is Millie. What are you dressed as?" Alice asked.

The green girl sniffled. "I'mdb mucus," she said, looking glum. She turned to Millie. "Are you fromdb Standish?"

"I'm camping with my family, on the other side of the lake," Millie said. She couldn't believe she was actually talking to not just one but three No-Fur girls, and that, so far, they seemed to be accepting her as one of their own. Except the one all in white, who was studying her curiously.

"That's an amazing costume," she said, walking in a slow circle around Millie, who felt her fur begin to bristle. The girl reached out to stroke her, and Millie forced herself not to flinch or tell the other girl—Riya, she thought—how rude it was to touch someone's fur without permission. "Where's the zipper?" Riya asked.

"Sewn into the seam," Millie squeaked.

"She's an Ewok," Alice said curtly. Millie sensed something, some mixture of fear and sympathy in the other girls' attitude toward Alice, the way they seemed to choose their words carefully when they talked to her, the way they held their bodies.

Alice isn't like them, Millie thought, and for some reason the idea gave her a thrill. She liked the idea that Alice didn't belong entirely to the No-Fur world, that she belonged, instead, to Millie.

The four girls approached the first of the learning guides' cottages. "Trickb-or-treatdb!" called Taley, knocking on the door. It was opened by a soft-voiced, mild-looking person named Clem, who praised their costumes and offered them carob-coconut bars, before frowning at Riya. "I thought Phil and Lori said no weapons?"

"I have permission," Riya said crisply . . . but when he'd shut his door she'd smiled and said, "Actually, I don't."

Millie held open her sack, accepted her treat, and with Alice by her side, and with Riya and Taley arguing aloud whether Riya's everyday fencing gear constituted a costume, trotted off in a swelling crowd of No-Fur kids dressed as clowns and peacocks and ballet dancers and mummies and things Millie couldn't begin to identify. The boys were whooping as they ran from cabin to cabin; the girls were chattering, complimenting each other on their hair and their clothes. As a girl strutted by in high heels, followed by a pair of giggling bedsheet ghosts, Millie, feeling nervous, grabbed Alice's hand.

"Are you okay?" asked Alice, who looked puzzled but friendly and nice. *She won't hurt me,* Millie told herself. *She's not like they say.*

"I am okay," said Millie, and made herself let go and follow Alice up the three steps and onto a seat on the school bus, which roared to life and went lurching down the road. The boys were singing, "Ninety-nine bottles of root beer on the wall," and the girls were pulling mirrors out of purses and pockets to inspect themselves. Millie shut her eyes and leaned her head back against the pebbled plastic of the bus seat, trying to make her knees stop quivering, thinking that working her way into No-Fur society was the first necessary step toward her eventual stardom.

I made it. I'm here, she thought. *I'm really here.*

CHAPTER 16

Alice

FOR ALICE IT WAS THE BEST HALLOWEEN THAT she could remember: running through the streets, shouting and laughing, with the crisp air reddening her cheeks and her bag sagging with candy, with her friend at her side.

In the crush of kids in costume, none of the learning guides noticed that Millie was a stranger or asked where she'd come from or if she had permission to be there. Alice enjoyed a pleasant daydream that she could keep her costume on and it would make her actually invisible; that she could slip through the world unseen and unnoticed until she found a place where she felt welcome.

At eleven o'clock the learning guides herded the kids back onto the bus. Alice and Millie sat down on a seat together behind Riya and Taley. Alice had always thought there was something a little strange about Millie, about the way she spoke, and how shy she was about letting Alice see her, and that night it was even more noticeable: the way she kept looking around, staring at Riya and Taley like she was trying to memorize everything about them, the way she'd lean toward them or toward Jessica Jarvis and her crew, like she didn't want to miss a single word they were saying. It was almost as if she'd never seen people before. But, of course, she hadn't seen many people, Alice thought. She'd been homeschooled in a small town with kids in the same religion. Of course this was all weird and strange.

Alice looked out the window and sighed, and she and Millie said, "I wish," at the exact same moment.

Alice looked at her friend. "You wish what?"

"I am wishing I could be in a place like this, with people." Millie's eyes—Alice saw that even her eyelids were furry—were half-shut, her mouth curved in a sweet smile. "I am wishing my mother and father would let me . . . you know." She gestured at the kids on the bus. "I am wishing they'd let me do things like this, with other kids. Different kids, not just Yare ones. I am wishing they'd let me go."

"Tell me more about your town," she said to Millie, hoping to change the subject. She realized, as she said it, that there was a lot she didn't know about her new friend, including her last name or the exact location of where she lived when she wasn't camping.

"Oh, it's just a regular kind of place," said Millie, waving one furry hand toward the window. Alice wondered how she'd gotten fur to stick on her hands. Spirit gum?

Millie, meanwhile, was unzipping her backpack. "I am so hungry," she announced. "Are you hungry?" She handed Alice a sandwich made with bread that looked homemade and took one for herself.

Alice took a bite, then closed her eyes. The jam tasted like essence of blackberries, sweetened with real sugar, not honey or maple syrup, which was what the Center usually used. Except for Kate's secret stash, there was no white sugar anywhere in the kitchen, and the learners usually had fruit or granola for dessert. "This is so good."

"It's blackberry jam," said Millie, who was talking with her mouth full. She swallowed, wiped her lips, and said, "My mother and I pick berries every summer and we put up jam ourselves."

Alice bit into the fresh bread and the sweet jam, humming with pleasure. Millie smiled, and Alice smiled back, and Millie started her chatter, describing some episode of *Friends* where Chandler's name was misspelled on the label of his *TV Guide*. Alice could feel herself relaxing, her shoulders descending from their usual spot up around her ears, her belly unclenching, her fingers resting loosely in her lap instead of forming fists. She never felt like Millie was making judgments about her broad shoulders and big feet and wild hair ... or that, if she was judging, she was deciding in Alice's favor. She'd complimented Alice's size and strength and speed so many times, had been so open in her admiration about Alice's body, that Alice could almost believe Millie was telling the truth and that the way Alice looked and acted were okay.

Besides, Millie was constantly saying that Alice had saved her life. "You couldn't have done that if you were some weak little puny wisp," she'd say. That gave Alice a warm, happy glow, a feeling that, maybe, for the first time in her life, she had found a friend, someone who liked her because she was who she was. Not Lee, whose job it was to drive her; not Riya and Taley, who had to be polite because they lived so close together; and not her granny, who was obligated to love her because they were related, but a real friend.

"Try these," Millie said, passing Alice more neatly wrapped packages, which turned out to be buttermilk doughnuts and dried plum hand-pies with wedges of goat cheese.

"Oh my God," sighed Alice. "This is the best food I've had in forever."

Millie, who always had a hundred questions, inquired, "What are your favorite snackles?"

"Well, now they're hand-pies," Alice said. "At home, all Felicia lets me have are baby carrots and grapes. At school we usually just get hummus." She frowned, thinking first about the garlicky beige glop that had tasted okay the first five or six times they'd served it and now felt like mortar in her mouth; then about the way her mother would watch her, perching casually on one of the chairs at the breakfast bar and trying to pretend she wasn't taking note of every single thing Alice ate.

"But that's terrible!" said Millie.

Alice, laughing, asked, "Do you want to hear the menu at the Center?" When Millie nodded, she said, "For breakfast every day we get whole-grain cereal with raisins."

"I hate raisins," said Millie with a shudder. "They are, like, grapes that something terrible has happened to, and instead of being grateful that they survived, they're just shriveled up and mad."

"I don't like them either," Alice said. "But at least they're a little sweet. Lori and Phil don't believe in refined sugar."

"They don't believe in eating it or don't believe it exists?" asked Millie.

"Oh, they believes it exists," said Alice, who'd heard from Kate that Lori kept a secret stash of chocolate-covered orange peel in a locked desk drawer in her office, "but they don't believe it's good for us, so we're not allowed to have any sweets."

"That," said Millie solemnly, "is a tragedy."

"I know," said Alice.

"Tell herdb aboutdb lunch," said Taley, who, along with Riya, had turned around to join the conversation.

"For lunch," said Alice, warming to the task, "we get tofu pups or soy-cheese sandwiches. Which would be fine, except we make our own whole-grain bread, and it's so crumbly that you can barely slice it, and it tastes like you're chewing the stuff they fill pillows with." She felt bad, like she was betraying Kate with her complaints, and the truth was that she didn't really mind the food that much, but she knew from her time with Jessica's crew that girls thought she was funny when she was mean.

"What about desserts?" asked Millie.

"Ha!" said Riya.

"Once in a while we get homemade granola. With raisins," Alice sighed. "For dinner we have lentil soup on Mondays, split-pea soup on Tuesdays, zucchini casserole on Wednesdays, tuna-noodle casserole on Thursdays, baked fish on Fridays, loaf on Saturdays . . ."

"Loaf?" Millie interrupted. "What's loaf?"

Alice shrugged. "Loaf is loaf. It's in the shape of a loaf."

"Some kids think it's meat loaf," said Riya. "Or lentils that look like meat."

"Once," said Taley, "itdb tastedb like salmon."

"Some kids think it's turkey loaf," said Alice. "And sometimes it's just more zucchini."

Millie drew herself up to her full height. "That," she said, "is unspeakable."

Alice nodded and waited until Taley and Riya had turned around before saying, "Can I ask you a question?"

"You just did!" said Millie, which was a joke her father often made with her.

Alice leaned close and lowered her voice. "The night we met . . . were you just going for a swim, or were you running away from home?"

Instead of answering, Millie smoothed the fur on her

arms, then fiddled with her hood, then bent down to zip up her backpack. "I wasn't exactly running to away. I was exploring. I like to be by myself sometimes," she said with such forcefulness it was as if she thought Alice had contradicted her. "But I'm never allowed. My parents follow me everywhere. They are never letting me alone."

Alice felt her face go soft with yearning. She imagined Felicia turning away from her mirror and her charity board meetings and her Pilates reformer, turning to Alice and saying, *Want to take a walk in Central Park? Want to go to the farmer's market and get blueberries? Want to bake a pie?* Her mother gave her presents, fancy things that Alice knew were expensive, but Alice didn't care about cashmere sweaters or gold necklaces. All she wanted was Felicia's time.

"My mother's bad. My papa's even worse," Millie continued. "He's always checking up on me. Stopping by my school if it's a school day. Sticking his head in at the house if I'm home. Going down to the lake to watch me swim."

"Helicobpter parents," snuffled Taley, who'd been listening. Millie nodded. Alice sighed.

"My parents don't see me at all. That's why I'm here. If I had parents like yours—parents who actually wanted me around—I'd . . ." *Never leave them,* she started to say, but couldn't get the words through the thickness in her throat.

"But what if they loved you, only they didn't understand you?" Millie asked. "What if they loved you but they never let you do the things you wanted to do?"

The bus made a sharp turn, bumping onto the dirt road that led to the Center. Millie peered through the window, up toward the cloudy sky. "What time is it?" she asked as the bus bounced over a pothole.

"Almost midnight," Alice said.

Looking alarmed, Millie snatched up her backpack and jumped to her feet. "I need to go," she said. Her eyes were open wide, and her fur looked somehow fluffier.

Alice felt her shoulders resume their hunch, and her belly get tight. Riya and Taley were nice enough, but they weren't her friends. Jessica and Christy and Cara had tricked her into thinking they liked her. What if Millie was tricking her too? What if she'd get off the bus, pull off her costume, revealing herself to be just as pretty as Jessica Jarvis, and say, "Ha, you dummy, did you actually think we were friends?"

Alice squeezed her eyes shut as the bus bounced over another pothole and started groaning up the dirt road that led to the Center. The learning guides were big on what Lori called "positive self-talk." Every morning Alice brushed her teeth and washed her face looking into a mirror with the words "You Are Loved and Special" painted in purple on the frame. Every day at least one of the learning guides, usually Clem or Kendra or Kate, would tell her that she'd done something wonderful, whether it was writing a haiku or whipping cream into perfect peaks or finding a runaway goat. But she didn't *feel* loved, and she never *felt* special. At least, not until she'd met Millie.

"Ouch!" Millie shouted.

Alice turned and saw Millie cringing away from Riya, cradling one of her hands in the other. Riya was staring at Millie, looking shocked.

"Sorry," Riya said.

"What happened?" asked Alice.

"Riya pulledb Millie's furdb," said Taley.

"I wanted to see how it was attached," Riya said.

"It's glue," said Millie. "And it's very rude to be pulling someone's fur without permission." She'd twisted her body away from the girls, and she was holding her hand like it really hurt. Alice saw that she'd painted her fingernails black, to make her hands look like Ewok paws. In fact, her hands really did look like Ewok paws . . .

Millie must have noticed her staring, because as soon

as the bus came to a stop, she pushed her way to the front and bolted out the door.

"Wait!" Alice called through the bus's open window. Millie was already running down the path. *If she thinks she's slow,* Alice thought, *the rest of the Yare must be ready for the Olympics.*

"I have to go," Millie called over her shoulder, running until she was only a shadow, like a gray ghost darting in and out of the trees.

Alice scrambled off the bus and stood staring helplessly, feeling the hand-pies turning to stones in her belly, her pillowcase dangling from her hand, as her friend disappeared. She wondered at Millie's strange hands with their long, curved black nails and how, in spite of what Millie had said, Alice hadn't been able to spot a zipper anywhere on her costume, no matter how carefully she'd looked.

"Hey, Al, did you lose your girlfriend?" Jessica Jarvis sang.

"Yeah, where's your fuzzy widdle teddy bear?" one of the Steves jeered.

"Leave her alone," said Riya.

"Oh, sticking up for the freak?" asked Jessica in an arch voice, as if this was the most amusing thing she could imagine.

Alice decided she'd heard enough. She dropped her

candy and ran into the darkness after Millie, ignoring the shouts of the learning guides and her classmates' laughter, ignoring Riya's and Taley's calls, ignoring even her own thoughts and the realization that she had absolutely no idea what she'd do if she managed to catch up with Millie; no idea what she'd say except for *Why did you take off like that*, and *I thought you were my friend.*

Alice ran faster, her legs devouring the distance. She ran until she couldn't run anymore, until the cramp burning in her side made her feel like she'd pass out if she took another breath. She stopped, gasping, with her hands on her knees, bent over, with the taste of copper in her throat. When she caught her breath, she raised her head.

"Millie! MILLIE!"

High up above, an owl hooted, and the wind rattled a tree's leafless branches. The moon was still hidden behind the clouds, and it was so dark that Alice could hardly see her own arm stretched out in front of her. She could smell dying leaves and feel the chill of the wind, announcing that summer was over and winter was coming. And what if Millie had fallen in a stream or snapped her ankle in a hole and was lying somewhere, helpless?

The wind gusted, pushing the clouds away. Silvery moonlight spilled down, illuminating the forest floor.

"Millie!" she called again, feeling angry and helpless. "MILLIE!"

She paced in circles, calling her friend's name, even though she knew that Millie was gone and that she'd never see her again. Finally, Alice pulled off her hat and put it down next to a tree.

"Good-bye," she whispered. "It was nice to have you as my friend."

She was walking away when a small, apologetic voice from above said, "I'm up here."

CHAPTER 17

Millie

MILLIE HAD RUN OFF INTO THE FOREST, hearing her mother's voice in her head as clearly as she heard Alice's shouts in her ears. *Now you've done it,* Septima's voice said. Millie's feet were blistered from their too-big boots, her throat ached, and her cheek was bleeding where a branch had smacked hard enough to cut through the fur.

Even while she ran, she could hear Alice calling. *Not calling, hunting,* Septima's voice whispered in her head, and, *Didn't I tell you? Didn't I warn you? Now look at you. Now look.*

Millie ran faster and faster, as fast as she'd ever gone . . .

and the Yare were, normally, very fast. But Millie was a very small Yare, with short legs and small feet, and Alice was tall for a human girl, tall and strong and determined. Millie's lungs were burning, and she suspected that she'd lost a fingernail somewhere . . . and what if Alice had a gun? Even though that guide person had said that none of the trick-or-treaters could carry even pretend weapons as part of their costumes because the Center didn't allow it, Millie had been taught that all No-Furs had guns and that they shot each other all the time, accidentally or on purpose. If Alice caught her and shot her and took her to a zoo, it would be nobody's fault but her own.

"Millie? MILLIE!"

She could hear Alice's voice getting louder. She threw herself at a tree, and then, clawing at the bark, she started to climb. *They will chase you and they will catch you and they will hurt you,* her mother's voice said.

"Millie! Please!" Alice called.

Millie crouched like a treed cat, cheek-fur matted and sticky with blood and sap, her candy—all of that delicious No-Fur candy—lost somewhere below. Frozen in fear and indecision, she clung to the topmost branch of the tree, looking down at Alice, who was standing below in the dark. She squinted, trying to spot the gun, but if Alice had one she'd hidden it well. In the moonlight, Millie could see Alice pacing, could hear muttering and noises that sounded like crying.

Finally she watched as Alice put her hat down at the base of the tree. "Good-bye," she heard the No-Fur girl whisper. "It was nice to have you as my friend."

That was when Millie made up her mind. Maybe No-Furs were dangerous. Maybe they did have guns. Maybe they did want to trap and kill the Bigfoots they found, or put them in zoos or sell them to the circus for money. But not Alice. Alice had saved her from drowning, and Alice had been kind. Alice had taken Millie trick-or-treating, and even though she was fast and strong, she always slowed down and never made Millie hurry to keep up. Alice had answered all her questions, had been honest about herself, had listened and not laughed when Millie told her about her dreams.

Alice was her friend.

"I'm up here," she called, and held her breath, and hopped down from the tree and stood, waiting for Alice to turn around and see her, really see her; waiting to say who, and what, she really was. She held herself perfectly still as Alice stared at her in silence.

"You didn't take your costume off," Alice finally blurted.

"This isn't a costume," Millie said. "This is how I really look. I am Yare. What humans call a Bigfoot."

There was a long pause.

"You're a Bigfoot?" Alice said.

"Yes," said Millie, who was trembling all over. "But only a small one."

"But Bigfoots aren't real!" Alice exclaimed. Then, glancing down, she said, "And your feet aren't even that big!"

"Nyebbeh! They are quite big enough!" said Millie, who disliked it when people made fun of her feet. "And we are real. There are a great many of us. But the No-Furs never see us. We live deep in the forest and we keep ourselves to ourselves, because," she said, and paused for a breath, "the No-Furs would shoot us if they found us." She looked at Alice, trembling even harder. "Are you going to shoot me? Please don't shoot me."

"Shoot you?" said Alice. "Why would I shoot you?"

"Because that is what No-Furs do to my people," said Millie.

"What is a No-Fur?" asked Alice, who looked slightly dazed, like something heavy had landed on her head. "Is that what you call us?"

"What else should we call you?" said Millie.

"Humans," said Alice. "Human beings."

Millie lifted her chin. "You are not beans. You are Yare with no fur," she said. "No-Furs."

Alice looked at Millie, and then reached out tentatively toward her hand. "Is it okay if I touch it?"

"Go ahead," said Millie. Alice patted her fur gently.

"So this is how you look all the time? It's not a costume?" Millie nodded. "This is me."

Alice looked amused and bewildered and more than a little bit hurt. "Why didn't you tell me?" she asked. "Why didn't you tell me that this is what you are?"

"Would you have believed me?" asked Millie.

Alice opened her mouth, then shut it. "I don't know," she said.

"Besides, I couldn't," Millie said. "You don't understand. We are not even supposed to talk to the No-Furs. You are not supposed to know we exist! There are No-Furs who hunt Yare, who would put us in zoos or in cages if they catch us. And," she said, gulping a deep breath, "I knew that if I told you, you wouldn't like me." She gulped down more air, feeling dizzy, her heart pounding, toes curled in her borrowed boots, cold sweat trickling through her fur. "You'd hurt me, or you wouldn't want to be my friend."

"I would never hurt you," Alice said.

"I know you wouldn't," said Millie. "I didn't know it at

first. But I know it now." She pictured Alice starting a new school in a new town or city every September, squaring her shoulders and facing off with girls she knew wouldn't like her. "You're the nicest No-Fur I ever met."

"I'm the only No-Fur you've ever met," said Alice. "I am, right? Do people look funny to you?" she asked, and answered her own question. "We must. We must look . . . naked."

Millie giggled. Alice smiled. Mille laughed. Alice laughed too, and then Millie grabbed her hand.

"I'm sorry I ran away," she said. She shot another worried glance toward the sky. "But now I must go. My parents will . . ." She smiled, using a phrase that Alice had taught her. "They will freak out because I've been gone so long."

Alice squeezed Millie's hand. "I'll go with you," she said.

Millie's eyes widened with alarm. "You can't," she blurted. "If I was bringing a No-Fur to the village . . . if anyone found out that I'd even been talking to you . . ."

"What would they do?" asked Alice.

"I don't know. Something bad." Millie bent her neck and mumbled into her fur. "Set my feet on the road." She lifted her head and looked at Alice, big, strong, beautiful Alice with her lovely thick reddish-blond hair. "You won't tell?"

"No," said Alice. Then she asked, "Do Bigfoots eat people?"

"Of course not!" said Millie. "We eat jelly sandwiches." As if to punctuate the remark, her stomach growled, making both girls laugh again. "Maybe we should be having a small snackle before I go," she said, and reached into her packsack.

Together the girls munched jelly sandwiches and cheese and pickles, and exchanged questions. Alice wanted to know if the proper plural was "Bigfoots" or "Bigfeet" ("Yare." "Bigfoot," Millie explained, was terribly insulting), whether they ever used to eat humans (no), and why they lived in forests (afraid of people).

Millie asked whether all humans had guns (no), whether there were laws about all No-Fur women all having to look the same (Alice said there weren't laws, but that being thin with long hair and high heels and makeup was strongly encouraged), and why people hunted Yare (Alice wasn't sure but promised she would look it up on the Internet).

"Tell me about your parents," Alice said as Millie helped herself to dried plums.

"Their names are Maximus and Septima. My papa is the Leader. He's very big but very gentle. My mother says that her job is taking care of me," said Millie. "Most Yare are afraid of No-Furs, but my parents—my mother especially—are, like, obsessed," she said, borrowing another turn of phrase she'd learned from Alice. "My ma tells me terrible stories about the things the No-Furs do to Yare if they catch them."

"Like what?" asked Alice, who loved all kinds of stories. "What stories does she tell?"

So Millie told her the tale of Bad Red-Suit No-Fur, and Alice started laughing. "But that's Santa Claus!" she said. "He isn't bad! He goes down the chimney to bring children presents, not steal things!"

"That is not what they tell us," Millie said sternly. "A No-Fur who can fit down chimneys is scary . . . and even his name sounds scary. Santa Claws!"

Alice laughed, shaking her head, and explained how "Claus" was spelled. When Millie told the story of the Bad Fairytooth No-Fur, Alice laughed even harder.

"That's the Tooth Fairy! And she doesn't take money from children! She takes their teeth, but only after they've fallen out, and she leaves money and a note under the pillow!" Alice paused, and sounded sad when she said, "Or sometimes your family's housekeeper just gives you a gift card."

As the moon rose higher in the sky, Millie ate, and Alice asked questions, dozens of questions. What did Yare houses look like? (They were made of sod, dug into hillsides, with cleverly vented chimneys that dispersed smoke throughout the forest.) Did Yare wear clothes? (Yes, but not always.) Drive cars? (Just once a year.)

Alice barely paused to take a breath. Did the Yare have pets? Did they ever take vacations? Did they ever have anything to do with the No-Furs? Like, for example, if they found a No-Fur baby abandoned in the forest, would they take it in and care for it and raise it with their own? Or if, just maybe, a lost No-Fur child came wandering through the woods and had no parents—or, at least, no parents who particularly wanted her back . . .

Millie pressed her lips together. Regretfully, she shook her head. "The Yare are scared of No-Furs. They'd never even touch a No-Fur baby. The only time we even go near the No-Furs is on Halloween, and when my father does the Mailing, and even then he is ever so careful."

Alice seemed eager to ask more, but Millie got to her feet, carefully brushing the crumbs from her fur. "I really, really must to go."

"Okay," said Alice. Millie heard her voice crack, could see the unhappiness on her face. She thought about Alice's life at the Center and horrible Jessica Jarvis and how every year was different but the same. Different schools, different girls, but the same scorn and misery. Different kids pulling different pranks, a dozen versions of Jessica Jarvis pointing and laughing, different Novembers where she'd watch her classmates depart for train stations and airports while she stayed behind at school because her parents were traveling and she wasn't invited to come along.

How would it feel to find out that there was another world out there, a world beneath the world, hidden away like the secret caramel center of a chocolate or a pearl tucked in an oyster's shell? A world where Alice could be accepted, even loved? To know that the world existed, but that she could never go there, that the doors would always be locked against her . . . Millie didn't want to think about it.

She stood, stretched out her arms, and gave Alice the biggest, hardest hug she could manage; then she said, "Good-bye," and kissed her friend's cheek and went running into the forest, toward home.

CHAPTER 18

Jeremy

DRESSED ALL IN BLACK—BLACK JEANS, A BLACK sweatshirt, a knitted black cap pulled down to cover his hair, and a black mask obscuring his face—Jeremy Bigelow began his Halloween crouched outside the gates of the Experimental Center for Love and Learning.

"Pay attention to the school," the old man on the phone had rasped. Jeremy had assumed he'd meant the middle school, and for the week after the call, he'd gone to school an hour early and spent that time, plus recess, scrutinizing the playground, the paths, the parking lot, the athletic field, and the woods behind them. After five days of looking, Jeremy hadn't found a thing, except for a few cigarette butts and an old deflated soccer ball. So he expanded his search, spending a day apiece at the town's three elementary schools and devoting a weekend to the high school—scouring the grass, examining the trees, collecting discarded soda cans and granola-bar wrappers with the plan of checking them later for fingerprints. He hadn't found a single scrap of evidence or encouragement and was starting to wonder if "school" could mean preschool or the Standish Academy of Karate or even the new yoga studio on Main Street, when he remembered hearing his parents talk about some kind of experimental school that had opened in the former campground on Lake Standish that fall.

Google led him to the school's website ("The Experimental Center for Love and Learning: a safe space where a community of committed learners comes together to explore the world"). Google Maps showed him precisely where the Center was located; Google Earth displayed pictures of the log-cabin-style dining hall, the dozen little cabins, and a wooden gate with what looked like driftwood and twigs spelling out the words "All Are Welcome Here" at the top. Jeremy had rolled his eyes, packed a bag, and headed out after dinner.

"I'm going trick-or-treating!" he called to his parents in the living room, even though they hadn't asked where he was going, hadn't seemed to notice that he wasn't wearing a costume, and didn't seem particularly interested in when he'd get back.

"Have fun, dear," said his mother.

"Be careful," said his dad.

He checked in with Jo, climbed on his bike, which he had reassembled, and pedaled through town, then along the bumpy dirt path that led to the Center. When he reached the gate he'd seen in the picture, he ditched his bike in the tall grasses and continued his trek on foot. The sign might have read "All Are Welcome Here," but Jeremy felt certain that a strange kid caught creeping around the grounds would not be welcome at all.

He could hear noises coming from the dining hall, the clatter of silverware and the hum of conversation. He watched and waited until the students started to leave, and then he tucked himself under the eaves of the building with his phone cupped in his hand. Kids in costumes streamed past—superheroes and ghosts, football players and devils and a girl all in green who kept sneezing—but they all just looked like regular kids. Then a broad-shouldered girl whose curly hair was pulled into a braid as thick as Jeremy's forearm walked by. The girl wore a trench coat and a hat with a brim and walked with her hands in her pockets. There was something about the way she stood, the defeated slump of her shoulders, the furtive way she looked around from the corners of her eyes, that reminded him of something—or someone—but he wasn't sure what.

Jeremy watched the girl look to her left and her right, then start walking swiftly down toward the lake . . . and, because he didn't have a plan, or any better ideas, he decided to follow her.

He stayed out of sight as she walked down to the lake, noticing the way she straightened up, held her head higher, and looked excited instead of ashamed as she got closer to the shore. "Millie! You're here!" he heard her call as a canoe glided onto the shore and a small, furry, gray creature that looked like a baby bear hopped out.

"Are you an Ewok?" he heard the bigger girl ask.

"An Ewok!" the canoe girl replied . . . and they walked off together, to go trick-or-treat at the cabins with the rest of the Center's students.

Ewok, thought Jeremy, snapping off shots as fast as his night-vision camera could take them. *As if.* He heard his blood thunder in his ears, felt himself flush with triumph as he tweezed a bit of gray fur that had drifted into the prickers. Then he ran to his bike and rode down back through town, weaving in and out of crowds of little kids dressed up like princesses and monsters, until he'd reached Jo's house.

She was, as always, in her Batcave, dressed in a Bikini Kill T-shirt and jeans and pristine sneakers—blue Nikes this time. More maps of Standish had joined the pushpin-studded original on the wall, along with half a dozen blowups of the side-by-side photographs, some with other Bigfoot illustrations superimposed on them.

"Jeremy," she said, spinning her Aeron chair around. "Whatcha got?"

"I got this," he said, and showed her the photographs of the girl and the furry creature, the clump of gray hair with a strand of reddish-blond that had gotten mixed in. Talking fast, trying to keep his story organized and concise, while leaving out, for reasons he didn't entirely understand, the weird telephone call he'd gotten—maybe because the old guy had been such a jerk, and also sexist—he told Jo that he'd started looking at schools and how he'd seen the big, broad-shouldered, sad-looking girl, and he'd followed her down to the lake, and seen the Ewok-quote-unquote.

Jo frowned. "It's awfully small," she said, studying the picture.

"Maybe it's a kid," Jeremy said. "A kid Bigfoot."

"Or a human kid in costume," said Jo.

"Or a kid Bigfoot," Jeremy persisted.

Jo smiled and slid across the floor, over to a bank of scanners and color printers set on shelves along one wall. In less than sixty seconds, she'd scanned the image, enlarged it, digitized it, overlaid it on top of the template of an average female human face, and set up a series of comparison points. Swiftly, red lines and dots formed a graph across the furry little face. Numbers raced across the bottom of the screen. Jo reached toward the image, pinched her fingertips together, then unbunched them, waving her hands like she was miming fireworks or a flower's bloom. The picture of the face expanded above Jeremy's head, outlined in gold, then shrank to a series of ratios and equations. Another *zzzzip* as Jo moved across the floor to play another computer's keyboard like a piano.

Jeremy, meanwhile, tweezed a single hair from the clump of gray. A drop of saline, a plastic slip, and the slides were ready to be clipped under the microscope's lens. Jo looked first, then waved Jeremy over. When he brought his eye to the lens, he could see that each slide showed a single hair attached to a bulb-shaped bit of flesh.

"I can do mtDNA here, but the stuff from the follicle— the stuff that'll really tell us what we've got—that's going to take longer." Jo said all this while typing at yet another computer, fingers rattling over the keys so fast that Jeremy was surprised the cursor could keep up.

"Okay, but what do you think?" he asked.

She peered into the screen for a long moment, then pushed him aside, gently, and looked down the microscope's lens once more. "It looks like fur from some kind of primate," she said.

"But . . . not human?" His heart was in his throat, his whole body thumping with its beats.

"Too soon to tell." Her voice was brusque, not unapologetic. She knew how badly Jeremy wanted this. "Could be a hoax. Let me send it to Lila."

Lila, Jeremy knew, was another one of Jo's friends, another member of the network of hunters. She was a nurse-practitioner turned stay-at-home mom who lived in Alabama and devoted her free time to Bigfoot hunting—specifically, sneaking samples into her hospital's lab and analyzing any blood, fur, footprints, or fingernail clippings to confirm that they came from human beings. "We'll wait and see."

Wait and see, thought Jeremy. He hated to wait. He wanted to see . . . and, as it happened, he didn't have to wait long at all.

He was sitting in Miss March's class the very next day, half paying attention to the lesson about the Louisiana Purchase, half beating himself up for not getting even a single piece of candy the night before, when the public-address system crackled with static, and the principal's voice said, "Jeremy Bigelow, please report to the principal's office."

Jeremy gathered his books, zipped up his backpack, and walked down the hall. The principal, Mr. Girardi, was waiting for him outside his office. His hands were clasped behind his back, and his face was grave.

"I'm afraid I have some sad news," he said. Jeremy made himself looked worried.

"Is it Grandma?" he asked.

Mr. Girardi put his hand on Jeremy's shoulder. "I'm so sorry," he said. "She passed this morning. Your parents said that you'll be leaving for the funeral immediately. You've got your bike, right? They need you home as soon as you can get there."

Jeremy hung his head so that Mr. Girardi wouldn't see his smile. He nodded. Mr. Girardi squeezed his shoulder.

"Please give my condolences to your family," the

principal said, and Jeremy nodded again and hurried out the door. He hopped on his bike and pedaled away, not toward his house, but to Jo's. This was their Bat-Signal, the one they'd agreed on months ago. Jo was home-schooled, and her time was her own, so if she needed him, and it was an emergency, she'd call the school pretending to be his mother and tell the principal that his grandmother (both of whom had actually died years before Jeremy was born) had died.

Stopping at a traffic light, Jeremy pulled out his phone. "Get here as fast as you can, I have news," Jo had texted. As soon as he finished reading that text, a second one arrived. "Hurry."

Jeremy felt his fingertips turn cold as the Town Hall bell tower tolled noon over his head. Jo never told him to hurry. In fact, Jo was usually telling him to slow down, to be thorough, to make sure he wasn't making sloppy mistakes. Jeremy pedaled faster than he ever had, and then dumped his bike on her lawn and raced to her lair.

Jo wore a baseball cap. Beneath its brim, her face looked pale and pinched. Her mouth was set in a straight line, and there were dark smudges underneath her eyes that suggested a sleepless night.

"Good news and bad news," she said, and Jeremy

heard the faintest quiver in her voice. He'd never heard Jo sound uncertain before, and he'd definitely never heard her sound afraid.

"Good news first?" he asked.

She managed a ghostly smile. "We got our first hit. The grayish fur you found . . . it's not from a human."

Jeremy heard his breath whoosh out of him. His knees started to tremble. His skin prickled with goose bumps. This was it. This was, as the old man had said, everything.

"And the bad news?" he managed.

Instead of speaking, Jo wheeled herself over to her desk, where a single piece of paper was waiting. "It came this morning," she said. "But not in the mailbox. I woke up, and it was on the floor outside my bedroom door."

Jeremy looked down, and felt his goose-bumped skin go icy. The missive, according to its letterhead, was from the Department of Official Inquiry, Paranormal Division. It was addressed to Miss Josette Taylor Tarquin and Master Jeremy Josiah Bigelow.

We have intercepted the samples you collected. We have copies of the photographs you have taken. Prepare to surrender everything related to your investigation, including but not limited to physical evidence, computer files, hard drives, disks, faxes, photographs, handwritten documents, and any and all correspondence. The courier will be at this residence at 0000 hours tomorrow, November 2. This is a matter of global security. We require your complete and total cooperation. If we do not receive it, penalties including but not limited to arrest and imprisonment will be assessed against you and your parents and/or guardians.

The letter was signed with an illegible flourish of black ink. The words "Matthew Carruthers, Director" were printed beneath it.

Jeremy picked up the sheet of paper. It was heavy, creamy, embossed with an image he couldn't see but could feel. Lifting the paper to the light revealed the imprint of a five-pointed star with the words "Department of Official Inquiry" written underneath it. Beneath the words was a drawing of a circle enclosed by an oval, and the motto *oculus videt in abscondito.*

"It's an eye," said Jo. Her voice was tiny. "And the Latin means 'The hidden eye sees all.'"

Jeremy felt a shudder work its way up his spine. "Is this real?" His lips felt numb, his tongue felt frozen. "This agency? Are we going to get in trouble?'"

"I can't find anything about the agency online, but the letter's real," Jo said. Her face was white, her forehead furrowed. She looked furious . . . and, he thought, beautiful in her anger. "Whoever broke into my house and left it for me was real."

"What do we do now?"

Jo gave him a smile like the edge of a knife. "Are you familiar with the expression 'sunlight is the best disinfectant'?"

Jeremy shook his head.

"It means we tell the whole world what we've found." Jo's mouth was set in a grim line. "November second isn't until midnight, so today—tonight—we let the whole world see. We put our pictures online. We tell everyone that the hair you found isn't from a human. We post to every group that has anything to do with Bigfoots or the paranormal. We call a press conference. We'll get the media there. If the whole world is watching, then this . . . this agency . . . it won't be able to hurt us. Especially because we're kids," she added, almost as an afterthought.

Jeremy shook his head. This was all too much, happening too fast. "Carruthers," he said. "Do you think it's any relation to Milford Carruthers?"

"I think that's the least of our concerns right now," Jo said, just as Jeremy's phone started buzzing against his hip. He pulled it out and saw a name he hardly ever saw flashing on the screen: Mom.

"Hello?"

"Jeremy?" His mother's voice was tight, higher than usual, and instead of her normal thoughtful tone, she sounded tense. Annoyed, he thought. Maybe even afraid. "Where are you?"

"At Jo's house," he said. "It's a half day. Teachers' in-service." His mother never paid much attention to the specifics of Jeremy's schedule, so she wouldn't expect him to be at school, but he gave her the excuse, just in case she was paying attention. "Why? What's up?"

"Can you meet me at Fitzsimmon's Market? My credit cards aren't working."

"What?" he said. Jo was staring at him. "Don't you have more than one?"

"Cards," his mother said. "Cards, plural. None of them

are working. Not my bank card, not my credit card . . ." She put her hand over the phone and said something sharp to the cashier. "Ugh. First my computer crashed—it wouldn't even restart, no matter what I did—and then I went shopping and *this* happened. I'm worried someone got my social security number and they've stolen my identity." She paused. "That's a thing, right? Identity theft?"

"I'll come with my allowance," Jeremy said. *Coincidence*, he thought, even as his mind was whispering more malevolent possibilities.

Jo tapped his shoulder. *What?* she mouthed. *My mom*, Jeremy mouthed back. "I've got my bike. I'll be there in ten minutes."

"Fine," said his mother . . . and then, to the cashier or the manager, "I promise you, I'm not trying to steal anything!"

"I'll be right back," Jeremy said as his mother hung up. Jo gave him a single, businesslike nod. On the screen, he saw the press release she'd already written. He scanned it quickly, seeing phrases like "compelling evidence" and "Standish has been a long-rumored site of Bigfoot activity" and "photographs and DNA evidence enclosed." On another screen, Jo had scanned in the pictures he'd snapped of the furry creature and was superimposing the Patterson-Gimlin stills over her body and face.

"If we hold this press conference . . . ," Jeremy began, thinking out loud. "People will start looking right away." Jo nodded. "So this Department of Official Inquiry will have people there, right?"

"Unless they're stupid," said Jo. "And I don't think they're stupid."

"Won't we lead them right to the Bigfoot?"

"Maybe we'll lead them," Jo said. "But we'll be there too." She gave herself a hard shove, pushing off from the desk and sliding her desk chair all the way across the lab and into the hall. Then she opened a coat closet, pulled out a folded-up arrangement of metal and wheels and gave it a single sharp shake. Jeremy watched, astonished, as the bars and leather resolved into a wheelchair, and Jo used her arms to hoist herself into it.

"Slipped capital femoral epiphysis," she said, pronouncing each word separately. "Unusual but not rare for adolescent females. It's where the head of the thigh bone isn't connecting correctly with the rest of the thigh bone, due to weakness at the growth plate."

"I'm sorry," Jeremy managed.

"Yeah, me too," said Jo. "It was misdiagnosed. My doctor kept saying it was just growing pains, and that I should stop complaining, and by the time my parents went for a second opinion . . ." She shrugged and started wheeling herself down the hall. "I've had two surgeries already, and I'll probably need more, and even then, they're not sure if I'll be able to walk or not."

"I'm sorry," he said again. This time she flashed him a thin smile.

"They're not sure," she said. "But I know I will. And it wasn't an awful thing. It was how I got into Bigfoot hunting in the first place. I had lots of time to kill in the hospital." Jo put her hand on his forearm and let it stay there for just a second. Jeremy felt the skin where she'd touched him thrumming like a hummingbird's wings. Then she reached down and gave the wheels a tiny flick, which sent the chair gliding toward the door.

Outside, the street was empty, except for a white van. The sign on its side read, "Standish Security Systems: Your Safety, Guaranteed."

"I bet," Jo murmured, as she took in the van. "Go give your mom her money first. Then we'll go for a ride. I emailed the press releases, but, just to be on the safe side, maybe we should take them to Channel Six and the *Standish Times* by hand, too."

"Of course," Jeremy said. *I'm scared,* he thought. But he was excited, too. This was real. It was going to happen. He, Jeremy Bigelow, had a friend, and the two of them were going to show the whole world that Bigfoots were real.

CHAPTER 19

Millie

THE MORNING AFTER HER HALLOWEENING adventure, the day after she'd revealed herself to Alice, Millie was in Old Aunt Yetta's house, reviewing the medicinal properties of turmeric, when the top-lap underneath her friend's bed gave a loud beep. Frowning, Old Aunt Yetta picked up her cane, made her way to the bedroom, bent down with a grunt, and retrieved the computer. Millie knew that her friend had set up special alerts and that the computer would beep anytime, day or night, that the word "Bigfoot" was mentioned in conjunction with terms like "Standish" and "upstate

New York" and even "Etsy." She watched as Old Aunt Yetta flipped the machine open, logged on, peered at the screen, and made a horrible choking noise.

"What?" Millie dashed over, trying to remember everything she'd learned about the Heimlich maneuver. Old Aunt Yetta pointed wordlessly at the screen.

"Bigfoots in Standish?" read the headline on the *Standish Times*'s website, in letters that seemed to scream off the page. There was the picture of Alice, naked and covered in pine needles and mud, next to the picture of Cousin Cassoundra, the one Old Aunt Yetta had already found on-the-line . . . only now it was in the local newspaper. Next to the shot was a pen-and-ink drawing of a Yare cringing in a cage, being displayed by a man in a fancy suit who was pointing at her with his cane. "Behold, LUCILLE, a FREAK OF NATURE," read the poster above her head.

And then, worst of all, there was a photograph of two blurry figures—one human, the other covered in silver-gray fur—making their way into the forest. Alice and Millie, at the Center, on Halloween.

Old Aunt Yetta was gasping, rocking back and forth with her arms wrapped around herself. Millie poured her a cup of water and leaned close to the screen, where she read about "Jeremy Bigelow, age twelve, a seventh grader at Standish Middle School," who said that he'd come across the first images online. Because he knew of Standish's "extensive history as the rumored home of Bigfoots," he'd started looking around . . . and near the "new and controversial alternative boarding school, the Experimental Center for Love and Learning," which had "opened its doors on the shores of Lake Standish in September" and had "already drawn scrutiny from the Board of Education due to its unorthodox teaching methods," he'd spotted two "mysterious figures" in the forest.

With a trembling finger, Millie pointed at the drawing of "Lucille" in her cage. "Is that . . . was she . . . ?"

"Yes," Old Aunt Yetta whispered back. "A Yare from long-and-long ago."

Millie kept reading. The article went into the history of Bigfoots in Standish, mentioning Milford Carruthers and the unfortunate Lucille. It discussed the Experimental Center for Love and Learning and said that Lori Moondaughter, one of the school's founders, had declined to be interviewed and refused to confirm or deny whether the pictures on the flyer had been taken at the school.

"Ms. Moondaughter, née Weinreb, emailed this

reporter a statement saying, 'We at the Center, as an intentional educational community, prize difference and celebrate the unique qualities that each of our learners brings.'"

Millie felt her stomach lurch, and her light breakfast of cinnamon toast, soft-boiled eggs, and apple turnovers threaten to reappear as she read the words at the bottom of the story: "Readers: If you have any information or sightings of your own to report, please contact Jeremy Bigelow at the email address below. The concerned citizens of Standish will hold a rally at the Lake Standish campground tonight at six p.m. to exchange information and discuss safety measures."

"Oh no," Old Aunt Yetta was muttering. "Oh no." Millie squeezed her eyes shut and started tugging at the fur on her cheeks. The campground was maybe a mile away from Alice's school and an easy paddle to the Yare encampment . . . if you knew where to go. And the picture, while blurry, was clearly a picture of her, and everyone in the Tribe would recognize it. Millie was the only Yare of her size, the only one with fur her color.

Old Aunt Yetta grabbed her cane, folded up the toplap, beckoned to Millie, and, without another word, went limping up the path to find Maximus. Within an hour everyone in the Tribe knew about the article and the planned rally and that it was Millie, in the company of a No-Fur, whose picture was in the paper, because Millie, disobedient as ever, had gone across the lake.

At noon the Yare assembled around the fire pit. Ricardan had a printout of the web page in one hand and the Speaking Stick in the other.

"You see," he hissed, almost before Maximus had finished the blessing. "You see? We should have left when they started building that school across the lake. And you," he said, pointing at Maximus, "*you* should have kept a tighter leash on that No-Fur-loving daughter of yours! Haven't we said that she'd be our ruination, with her singing and her talk about how the No-Furs could be our friends?" he asked, as Tulip nodded virtuously. "Didn't we say that she'd come to no good?"

Millie stood between her parents with her head hanging down. On her left, Septima clutched her apron and cried, her tears soaking her face-fur. On her right, Maximus stood stone-faced and silent. When Ricardan paused, Maximus took the Speaking Stick and pronounced the words that Millie had expected but dreaded. "We will be going. As quickly as we can. Pack what you can, and assemble Underground in an hour."

The Yare gasped. "Underground" was a tunnel, an ancient escape route for the direst of emergencies. It ran underneath mountains and ridges, and let out in a valley in another county ten miles away.

Old Aunt Yetta looked at the ground. Little Florrie started to cry, and then so did Frederee.

Millie slipped free of her mother's grasp and marched her small self to the center of the circle.

"This is my doing," she said.

Aelia nodded, and Frederee sniffled, and Ricardan actually bared his teeth.

"I went across the lake, and I met a girl, a No-Fur named Alice," Millie continued. "I know that I put us in danger, but I think I am knowing a way that I—that we— can make it right. If you'll let me talk to her—"

"Talk to her!" Melissandra whispered, in as loud a whisper as she could. "So the No-Furs can be taking more pictures of you? Or maybe the No-Fur will lead them right here!"

"Alice wouldn't do that!" Millie was shouting, and oh, it felt good to shout, to raise her voice until it echoed from the treetops and not worry about being shushed or punished. "Maybe most of the No-Furs are bad. Maybe most of them are having guns. But not Alice! Alice is a good egg! Alice is my friend!"

Shocked silence greeted this pronouncement. To call another Yare a "good egg" was the highest compliment you could pay . . . and to call a No-Fur a friend? The other Yare looked puzzled or angry. Poor Aelia looked like she was going to faint.

"Alice is my friend, and we can be fixing this," Millie said. A plan had started to form in her mind, not perfect, not yet, but the pieces, at least, were emerging. "We can be fixing it so they'll never find us. Not now, not for years-upon-years."

For a long moment there was silence. Finally Maximus said, "We can pack our things, but let Millie try her planning." Over the hisses and mutters of the other Yare, he bent low and whispered to Millie, "A Leader keeps her people safe."

Millie nodded. Part of her felt proud, but part of her—a much bigger part—was terrified. She'd never seen her father looking scared, had never even imagined that it was possible for Maximus, so big and brave and solid, to even be afraid.

Millie snatched the computer, praying that Alice was carrying her phone, and tapped out a message. Fifteen minutes later Alice had written her reply. Millie raced to the lake's edge to wait, and soon Alice in her kayak came paddling up onto the shore.

"Are you sure about this?" Alice whispered as she and Millie dragged the boat up to the woods.

Millie tried to smile. "In for a penny, in for a pounding," she said. "Besides, we have to try. Come on. I will make the introductions." She grabbed Alice's hand, and together the two of them trotted up to the Yare encampment, with Millie giving the occasional tug to get her wide-eyed friend to stop staring—at the gardens, at the sod houses, at the fire pit and the Lookout Tree—and keep moving.

Melissandra was the first of the Yare to see Alice. She sucked in a shocked breath, lifted her hand, and pointed, wordlessly, her mouth open in a silent scream, her fingers shaking. Ricardan yelped and ran off, leaving his terrified wife behind. Tulip just stared, mouth open, eyes wide.

"That went well," Alice said. She raised her hand at Frederee, who attempted his own wave back before he, too, freaked out and ran away . . . and then they were at Millie's house. Septima was in the kitchen, wrapping her best dishes in bits of burlap sacking. Maximus was looking through the narrow window as if he were trying to memorize the village he would never see again.

Millie cleared her throat. "Mother, Father, this is Alice," she announced, her voice sweet and clear and pure. "This is Alice, my friend."

CHAPTER 20

Alice

ALICE FELT A GLOW INSIDE OF HER, LIKE SHE'D swallowed a spoonful of sunshine. *Even if this all goes wrong,* she thought, *at least I will have had this. At least I will have had a friend.* She stepped forward, head back, shoulders squared, feeling braver than she ever had, ready to explain the plan that she and Millie had made . . . but as soon as she opened her mouth, Maximus's big hands grasped her shoulders.

"Wait," he said. "I will gather the Tribe."

A few minutes later, two dozen Yare, giant and hulking and covered in fur, were gathered in a circle. Maximus held a tall staff—the Speaking Stick, Millie had told her. Alice tried not to stare. She could feel their eyes on her, their gazes ranging from curious to distrustful to hostile. Fear twisted in her belly—they were all so big—and braided with the pity she felt for them. She knew what it was like to want to be invisible. She couldn't imagine, though, what it would be like if you had to hide, and disguise yourself all the time, because being seen meant danger or death.

She looked at Millie, who nodded. *She's my friend,* Alice thought. *I have to try.* "This is Alice of the No-Fur," Maximus began. "Will you hear her now?"

"We will hear," the Yare murmured, some more reluctantly than others.

Alice took one step forward, then another, and when Maximus handed her the staff, she wrapped her hand around it and leaned forward, letting it take her weight. The Yare watched, barely making a sound, each of their faces grave and intent.

"My name is Alice Mayfair," Alice said. "I'm a learner— a student—at the school across the lake. I'm sorry I got you in trouble . . . but Millie and I think that we have a way to help." She paused, gulped a breath of air, and squeezed the Speaking Stick hard, with both hands, so that no one would see her tremble.

The Yare were looking at her, examining her more

carefully than even Felicia and her fancy ladies-who-lunch friends ever had. But instead of looking to see whether she was dressed appropriately, whether her shoes were scuffed or her hair was tangled, they were looking to see if she was dangerous, if she had a gun, if she was going to hurt them. Alice felt another surge of sympathy, as she thought of how lonely and afraid they all must be, just as the youngest one—Florrie, she thought—raced forward and touched her hand.

"Florrie!" the little Yare's mother hissed, and yanked her daughter backward, in an agony of shame and fear.

Florrie giggled. "She's all bare!" she said. "All bare and nakedy."

"*Florrie!*" The Yare was tugging at her daughter's ear with one hand and covering her own eyes—in embarrassment, Alice thought—with the other.

"How did you find us?" Old Aunt Yetta asked in her cracked and screechy voice.

"You know how," growled Ricardan. "It's that Millie. Always having the curiosity, always asking the questions about the No-Furs. Always singing." He made the word "singing" sound like "murdering innocent kittens."

"It's not Millie's fault!" When all the Yare flinched, Alice lowered her voice. "Millie just wants to be who she is. It's not her fault she wanted to find people to be with, people who can appreciate her." She lifted her head and said, "I think I know how to fix this . . . but I need Millie's help. I need her to come with me, across the lake."

For an endless minute, the Tribe just stared.

"No!" Septima whispered. She was shaking so hard that Alice could see her fur tremble. She pulled Millie back against her body and held her daughter tight. "No, I won't have it. I won't risk her. She is my only cub, the only one I'll ever have, and I won't let her be hurt." She turned to the rest of the Tribe, her hair disarranged, her eyes wild. "We can go. We can go now. If we leave . . . leave our things behind . . . if we're being fast and quiet, they might not be able to catch us. . . ."

"Don't I have a choice in this?" Millie slipped out of her mother's grasp. She snatched the Speaking Stick.

"I am Millietta of the Yare. Would you hear me?"

For a moment the Tribe just stared. "We will hear," Maximus finally said, even though littlies were never allowed to speak at Tribe meetings.

Millie gave the Speaking Stick to Alice and turned to face both her parents, hands out in appeal. "If you raised me rightly, then I'll decide the right thing. And what I decide is to help my Tribe."

There was silence. Alice held her breath. Finally Maximus gave a single nod. "We will go to the tunnel for now. We will hide," he said. "Do what you can, Alice of the No-Fur. And, Millie . . ." He crouched down until he could look his little daughter right in the eye. "I believe in you," he said.

Millie nodded. Then she looked at Alice, indicating her fur. "Should I be disguising myself?"

"No," Alice said, and almost smiled, remembering the Experimental Center for Love and Learning's motto, the one spelled out on its website and on every piece of mail that it sent: "Where Every Child Is Special."

"Keep your fur. I want you just the way you are." She stood up straight, shoulders back, hair slipping free from its braid, and let the Yare look at her, examining her from the top of her head to the tips of her toes, as she explained what she had in mind.

Two hours later, Alice knocked at the entrance to Phil and Lori's office. Before they could invite her in, before she could lose her nerve and run away, she pushed the door open and pulled Millie inside.

Lori's mouth dropped open as she stared at Millie, whose furry face and arms and legs were left bare by her blue dress. Phil's guitar fell to the ground with an unlovely jangle. Alice couldn't help but be amused—they said they celebrated difference, but when they saw someone who was actually, genuinely not like them, they were just as scared as everyone else.

As she told the story that she and Millie had put together on their paddle across the lake, Phil tugged at his beard and Lori closed her mouth and pulled her reading glasses out of her needlepoint purse (purchased, she'd told the learners, on a trip to Guatemala and sewn by indigenous craftswomen who were paid a living wage).

"Explain that all again," Lori finally said. "Start from the beginning."

"This is my cousin Millie," Alice began, feeling a prickle of unease as she wondered how much time they had until the rally began. "She's got a genetic condition."

"Pilius lupus," Millie said (she and Alice had consulted an English-to-Latin dictionary on Alice's phone on their way to the office). "Basically it means I'm . . . well . . . you can see for yourself."

"My goodness," Lori murmured.

"Millie's parents were visiting Standish," Alice said. "They were thinking about bringing Millie to look at the

Center after I told them about it. So far she's just been homeschooled. My aunt and uncle tried public school, and then private school, but you can guess how that went."

"Children can be so cruel," Millie murmured with an exaggerated expression of sorrow. Lori made a cooing noise and Phil's face became stern. Alice could tell that, even in the midst of everything, Millie was enjoying her chance to interact with the No-Furs. Not just to meet them, she thought, but to perform for them.

"Not at the Experimental Center," Phil said. "We don't tolerate intolerance."

"That's what I told Uncle Max and Aunt Septi," Alice said. "They didn't want to let Millie even come for a visit. But I told them how you guys were, and how you made me feel, and how great you were about the whole . . . you know, the whole thing that happened to me. I said, 'This is a place where any kid can feel safe and happy and free to be her-self.'" This was the longest speech Alice had made to any-one at the Center, and she felt breathless when it was done.

Phil clasped his hands against his heart, trapping his beard against his chest. Lori's eyes were glistening. "Alice," she said. "I can't tell you how much it means to hear you say that and how much we value your faith in our community. We'll take good care of Millie. Don't you worry about a thing."

Alice and Millie nodded, and when Lori and Phil weren't looking, Alice gave Millie a wink.

"One other thing," Alice said. "On Halloween, Millie came trick-or-treating with me, and when we were in Standish, some kids in town saw her. They were staring and pointing, and I heard them say something about how she looked like a Bigfoot and how they should bring their friends to the old campsite tonight to look at the freak."

Phil's face hardened, and Lori's lips thinned. Alice saw the look they exchanged. She knew they'd been contacted by the paper and guessed they must have heard or read about the rally that night.

"Alice, you should have made sure we knew about Millie before you went trick-or-treating with her," Lori said. "But we won't worry about that right now. For now . . ." Lori bent down to sweep Millie into a hug that squished Millie's face against Lori's bosom. "Don't you worry about anything. We will keep you safe."

"You really think this will work?" Millie asked as she followed Alice toward Bunk Ladybug.

"We have to try," said Alice. She didn't know if it would

last, but for now all her nervousness and self-consciousness had magically disappeared, and left behind was a sense of resolve and courage.

When she opened the door, Riya was in the corner watching the 1988 Olympic fencing matches on her phone. Taley was in the bathroom with her replacement neti pot. Jessica was standing in front of the full-length three-way mirror she'd installed on the closet door, considering her outfit—a short skirt and cropped top—from three different angles.

"Hi, guys," said Alice. Riya put her phone down. Taley looked over her shoulder, with her steaming neti pot in her hand. Even Jessica stopped primping. Alice realized that in almost ten weeks of school, she couldn't remember a single time where she'd been the one to say hello to her bunkmates first. "Do you remember Millie?"

The three of them looked at Alice's fur-covered friend.

"You're stillbd wearing your costumebd," Taley finally said.

"I don't think it's a costume," said Riya.

Jessica sniffed and muttered something that sounded like "freak." Alice glared at her.

"Riya, you're right. Millie's fur wasn't really a costume. She has a rare medical condition, and she doesn't like people staring at her. . . ." She paused to give Jessica a dirty look. "Or making her feel different because of things that aren't her fault. Halloween's the only day of the year she even goes out in public. Only now," Alice continued, "some people from town saw her, and they're chasing her and trying to take her picture."

"Why do they wantbd to do thatbd?" asked Taley, reaching for a handkerchief.

"To put her picture online," said Alice, still giving Jessica a hard look. "To embarrass her and try to make her feel like she doesn't matter."

Jessica rolled her eyes. Millie gave Jessica a long and careful look, then bared her teeth and gave a very soft hiss. Jessica flinched.

"She needs our help," said Alice. "It's not her fault she's got"—she stopped herself before she said the word "fur"— "hair. It isn't catching, and she isn't dangerous. She won't hurt anyone; she's my friend, my only friend. . . ."

Alice closed her mouth. Riya was still staring. From the bathroom Taley sniffled. Then she asked, "Aren'tdb we your frienddbs too?"

Alice blinked. She knew that Jessica hated her. She had assumed that everyone else in the seventh grade, possibly everyone else at the Center, did too, and that Riya and Taley only put up with her because they had to. "I . . . I guess?"

"We want to be your friends," Riya said. "But you don't seem to like us very much."

"You dleave in the morndings and dyou won't tell anyone where you dgo," said Taley. Then she sneezed three times in a row. Millie looked alarmed. "I hdabe allergies," Taley explained. "Dust, bpollen, pet dander . . ."

"Why don't you just tell her what you're not allergic to? That would probably take less time," Jessica said, lifting her chin in the air.

Millie turned toward Jessica. "Nyeh," she said. "I know what you are." Her voice was very soft, but Alice could hear the dislike inside of it, like a fist inside the pocket of a fancy fur coat. She thought that Jessica heard it too, because, again, she flinched, then gave her hair a toss.

"I'm out of here," she said. Riya jumped up and stood in front of her.

"No," Riya said, "you're not. You owe Alice."

"I owe Alice what?" Jessica's expression was scornful, her glossy lips curled in disdain, but Alice could hear the faintest tremble in her voice. "It's not my fault she actually thought normal kids would want to be friends with . . ." There was a tiny pause. Alice saw Jessica's gaze slide toward Millie, who had her hands folded over her chest and whose fur seemed to be bristling. "With someone like her," she concluded.

"Normal kids," Millie repeated. Jessica attempted another head toss, but this one was far less emphatic, and she bumped her hip on the corner of the bunk bed and almost tripped on her way to the door. In a flash Riya was there, foil in her hand, standing between Jessica and freedom.

"Oh no, you don't," she said.

"Oh yes, I do, freak," Jessica sneered. Riya lifted her sword. Jessica cringed, then said, "Get out of my way or I'll tell Lori and Phil you've got a weapon in here."

"She's allowedb to havbe itdb," said Taley. "She's gotb sbecial permissiondb. Which you wouldb know," she continued, "if you didn't ignoredb us all the timebd."

"Great," Jessica muttered . . . and now Alice was positive that her nemesis looked afraid. "I'm not helping her," Jessica said. "I don't want any part of this."

"Oh, you don't have to do anything," said Millie in a silky, somehow dangerous voice. She smiled in a way Alice had never seen her smile before, a grin that displayed all of her very white and sharp-looking teeth, then repeated a line that Alice had used. "Just be yourself," she said.

CHAPTER 21

Jeremy

JEREMY'S TWEETS AND BLOG POSTS, THE BANNER headline on Believeinbigfoot.com, and the press releases he and Jo had delivered instructed people to gather at the old Lake Standish campground, which had a large parking lot and was an easy walk to the Center. His plan was to present his evidence—the picture he'd found online, then the picture he'd taken of the two girls and the fur that he'd collected, the fur that wasn't human hair. Then he would lead a contingent to the Experimental Center, while Jo, in the kayak they'd rented that afternoon, would lead the charge across the lake, in case the Bigfoot had fled the Center and was hiding out in the forest.

By six o'clock the parking lot was full, and a noisy, raucous crowd was gathered on the shore. Jeremy figured that maybe half the people were actually serious, either about spotting a Bigfoot or about protecting themselves. The rest were treating the night like a tailgate party or a football game. These were the ones who'd come with coolers instead of flashlights and with beers instead of the water bottles the press release had recommended. One group had even brought s'mores fixings and were building a bonfire. Jeremy paced along the edge of the parking lot with Jo, who was gliding along beside him in her sleek, low-slung red metal wheelchair.

"Do you see what I see?" she asked.

Jeremy turned toward where she was pointing and saw a News 6 van pulling down the dirt road, with the satellite dish on its roof practically brushing against the power lines. He swallowed hard as Donnetta Dale, wearing a dark-brown suit, a brown-and-gold scarf, gold earrings, and high-heeled shoes, stepped out of the passenger's side.

"Mr. Bigelow?" she called, peering into the twilight.

Jeremy gulped and dashed over, clutching a stack of press releases. "Right here," he said. If Donnetta Dale wasn't used to dealing with twelve-year-olds, the only evidence was a brief widening of her expertly shadowed eyes as she shook his hand.

"Do you have a copy of the images that we can use?" Donnetta asked. Jeremy did. Meanwhile, headlights were flooding the street; the Channel 10 News at Night truck was pulling in behind Channel 6. Trailing it were three cars and a dirty white van with a Phish sticker clinging to its rusty bumper . . . a van, Jeremy thought, that could have been easily disguised to look like a plumbing van or one that installed security systems.

He stared at the van until Donnetta Dale, who was even prettier in person than she was on TV, and also smelled good, put her hand on his shoulder.

"So you're a Bigfoot hunter?" she asked.

Jeremy, too nervous to speak, merely nodded.

"Thanks for doing such a thorough job on the background," said Donnetta. "I remember hearing stories about Bigfoots in the woods around Standish when I was a little girl. . . ." She gave a wry smile. "You know, back in the Mesozoic era. My gran used to tell me about how her father actually knew someone who was rumored to be half-Bigfoot. He had pictures and everything." She wrinkled her nose charmingly. "The guy could've just been tall and hairy, but I always wondered."

"Actually, there have been multiple reports, going back hundreds of years, about sightings in this region," Jeremy said.

Donnetta held up her hand like a crossing guard. "I'm going to stop you right there. I'd love to shoot some B-roll if that's okay. Hey, Bryan?" she called, and a cameraman came hustling over.

Jeremy smiled. There were people here, there were reporters here, his friend was here. People who believed him or who, at least, didn't *not* believe him were here. All he needed now was—

"Hey, man!" brayed a loud, slightly slurred teenage male voice. "Where are the Yetis?"

"Not Yetis, Bigfoots!" Jeremy heard Jo say. The guy and his friends—all of them, Jeremy saw with his heart sinking, had beers in their hands—ignored her.

"Bring on the Teen Wolf!" the young man yelled as his friends started to cackle, then to chant.

"Teen Wolf! Teen Wolf! TEEN WOLF!"

"Be quiet!" Jo was shouting. "Just listen, and we'll tell you what we found!"

"Shut up, kid!" said one of the guys, and then with a laugh he gave her chair a shove. Jo grabbed the wheels to stop herself but still came close to flipping face-first into

267

the dirt. Jeremy felt sick. He turned toward Donnetta Dale, the nearest grown-up, thinking that the adults would stop this, but Donnetta had gone over to her cameraman and was gesturing toward the yelling drunk people. As Jeremy watched, the cameraman turned on his lights and then, instead of telling the guys to cut it out and leave Jo alone, he started to film them.

Jeremy saw an empty pickup truck and jumped up onto its bed, banging his shin in the process. Tears came to his eyes. He wiped them away, looking for Jo, who'd gotten shoved to the back of the crowd.

He stood up. "Hey!" he yelled. "Hey, everyone! My name is Jeremy Bigelow, and if you'd all just give me your attention for a moment . . ."

The crowd's reaction was about the same as his class-mates' had been when he'd launched into his annual report on Bigfoots Are Real.

"Siddown, kid!" called one of the teenage boys.

"We came here to see the monsters!" said a sun-burned woman with curly blond hair and a tight pink top. "Where're the monsters?"

"They're not monsters!" Jeremy yelled. He heard his voice crack. "They're just different!" He wondered—too late, he knew—how many of these people had guns, how many of them had come not to find a Bigfoot but to hunt one. *They're the monsters,* he thought, staring down at the chanting, seething crowd. Jo's head was bent so that all he could see was the top of her baseball cap. *They're the monsters, and Jo and I are the freaks.*

"Look!" a woman shrieked. Jeremy peered into the twilight as the camera operators swung their lights in the direction the woman had pointed, flooding the forest in a brilliant glow . . . and then he saw it, a familiar hunched figure running out of the forest, about two hundred yards away from the beach, with big hands and big feet and a thick, curly, chestnut-brown pelt.

"There!" Jeremy yelled. "RIGHT THERE!" It wasn't the little gray-furred thing he'd seen—it was much bigger— but it was something. Maybe a friend or a relative, and it definitely wasn't human. Without looking to see whether anyone else was following, he leaped off the truck and started to run.

CHAPTER 22

Alice

ALICE, WITH HER HAIR UNBOUND AND HER feet bare, dressed in the furry brown vest that Taley had whipped up on her sewing machine, ran through the forest. She felt cold dirt and moss, dead leaves, and pine needles under her feet, and her breath burned her throat and lungs. Her legs ached. Her heart felt like it would burst. She made herself go faster, arms pumping, feet flying, spurred on by the sounds of people chasing her, and the lights from the TV cameras bobbing through the forest.

I can do this, she told herself, remembering how every morning she'd run through the woods alone and remembering that her friend—her friends—were waiting. Millie was counting on her. She would do this, or she would die trying.

They won't hurt me, she thought as she caught one ankle on a fallen tree branch and went sprawling on her face. The air went whooshing out of her. For a moment she couldn't breathe, couldn't move. Her furry vest had split along one seam, and her palms were bleeding. Then, as she heard her pursuers draw closer, leaves crunching and branches cracking under their feet, she forced herself to get up, then limp, then walk, then jog, then run. *All they've got are cameras,* she told herself as she ran in the direction of the Experimental Center for Love and Learning. *And I've already had my picture taken and posted all over school. It was even in the paper. I survived that, and I can survive this, too, if I have to do it to keep Millie safe.*

Her sides throbbed. Her lungs burned. She tasted hot copper in her throat as she made herself keep going, faster than she'd ever gone before. She scraped her shoulder on a protruding branch, snagged her sleeve in a pricker bush, slipped, and fell in a stream. With the stones bruising her knees and the cold water soaking her clothes and hair, she thought, *They're all going to stare at me.* The thought came wrapped in shame and horror—even in the cold, she felt her face start to burn—but she made herself get up, push forward, keep running. *For Millie,* she thought as she turned toward the Center. *For Millie.*

Once they'd come up with the plan, Alice had volunteered to be the lure. "What if they don't chase you?" Millie had said. "What if they just think you're—you know—a regular girl?"

"They'll chase me," said Alice with more confidence than she felt. "People see what they want to see. If they want to see a Bigfoot, then that's what they'll think I am."

"Do dbyou wantb a disguisbe? Sombde fur or something?" Taley asked. Her hazel eyes, behind her glasses, looked excited. Alice remembered how Taley had come up with Alice's Invisible Man costume, how she'd made the wigs and costumes for every one of the Center's plays and skits.

Alice thought, then said, "How fast can you make something?"

Taley was already reaching for the sewing basket that she kept in the corner, telling Riya to go to the drama closet and see if they still had the vests from the *Goldilocks and the Three Bears* play the Center had done the year before, where the moral, Alice remembered overhearing, was that all the chairs and beds and bowls of porridge were "just right." Meanwhile, Alice pulled her hair out of its braid, letting it spring into a curly thicket that covered most of her back.

"I bet that'll do it," she said. While Taley glue-gunned extra fur to a pair of mittens, Alice was breathing mindfully, the way Kara, who taught yoga, had shown them, pulling air in slowly through her nose, letting out through her mouth, trying to calm her racing heart. "Okay," Taley said. "All donedb."

Alice nodded. It was getting dark by then, and cold, with a thin crescent of moon visible in the indigo sky and the stars stabbing the darkness with pinpricks of silvery light. Alice thought of the rest of the Yare, huddled Underground, in their tunnel, waiting for word as to whether they could stay or if their feet would be set on the road.

She thought of what it felt like to be chased, laughed at, mocked, misunderstood, turned into a punch line, the butt of other peoples' jokes, all because you looked different.

She thought of Felicia, pressing her cool cheek against the top of Alice's head every time Alice left for a new school but not giving her an actual kiss, and the way her father wouldn't even look up from his phone when Alice came into the room, and her granny, saying, "You need to find your people." Her heart was a jumble of impulses: a desire to be brave and to keep Millie safe tangling with an impulse to run away from the danger, to go back to where the Yare were hiding, throw herself on their mercy, tell them, *Take me with you.*

"Alice?" Millie's voice was soft. "It's almost time." They'd decided to wait until after six for Alice to make her appearance. "Givdbe the crowdb time to getb excitedb," Taley had advised.

Alice nodded. She put on the vest and the furry mittens, and bent each arm, pulling them back behind her head, before lifting each ankle to stretch out her quads. She pushed past Jessica, jogged through the Center's gates, and moved toward the campground at an easy lope, until she heard the cars and the voices and saw the television camera lights.

Her plan was to shout until they saw her, but she didn't even need to open her mouth. First a woman screamed and pointed. Then the camera's lights picked her out of the gathering shadows. Finally Jeremy Bigelow—she knew it had to be him, even though she'd never seen him before—looked at her from where he was standing on top of a truck. For a moment their eyes met.

"THERE!" he shouted.

Alice turned and started to run the other way, leading the crowd away from the lake and the forest and the Yare . . . or, at least, all of them except one.

Millie, she thought as she led them toward the Center, *we better have been right. This better work.*

She dug down deep for the last scraps of her strength, for one final, desperate burst of speed. Her body gave it to her. The round, muscled thighs she'd always despaired of, the broad shoulders and big feet she hated, all of them worked together like a perfect machine, keeping Alice safely ahead of her pursuers. She sprinted through the Center's gates . . . and there, thank God, were Lori and Phil, with their arms crossed against their chests and identical stony expressions on their faces.

"Stop right there," said Phil as Jeremy pulled up, panting, and a crowd of first a dozen, then a few dozen, then maybe fifty strangers lined up behind him.

"This is private property!" Lori shouted as the first news van jerked to stop.

"And you are?" asked Donnetta Dale, patting her hair as she emerged from the News 6 van. Behind her a cameraman turned on his light. Lori squinted angrily, throwing one hand up to shield her eyes.

"Not that it's any of your business, but my name is Lori Moondaughter. I am one of the founders of the village that is the Experimental Center for Love and Learning. Alice—the little learner you're all chasing—is a member of our community. She is welcome here. You"—she raked the assembled crowd members with her gaze—"are not."

"We have reason to believe you may be harboring a dangerous creature," Donnetta said smoothly.

"Ridiculous!" said Phil. With his beard and his face paint, he looked as weird as Alice had hoped he would. "We are harboring—quote-unquote—a group of young explorers who've chosen to be here, of their own free will, as part of a communal experience in knowledge acquisition."

"I think that means it's a school," Alice heard one of the cameramen say. She leaned against the gatepost, gasping for air, afraid to even look at Millie. Off to the side, to the rear of the crowd, she saw Jeremy's head bent as he talked to a girl in a red wheelchair.

Donnetta Dale was as cool and composed as ever. "What do you have to say about this?" she asked, and handed Phil a piece of paper. Alice guessed it was the flyer Jessica and her friends had made, the one with her picture beside a Bigfoot's.

Phil barely glanced at it. "What I have to say is that

people are allowed, in this great nation of ours, to look any way they want to. I would say that conventionality is not morality, that conformity isn't a requirement, that individuality is not a crime, and that—"

"She's a Bigfoot!" screeched a woman in a pink shirt, pointing at Alice.

Phil's head shot up. Lori's eyes narrowed. The woman in pink wobbled forward, looking not entirely steady on her feet. Her face was flushed, and with every step, her chest jiggled under her tight shirt, and beer splashed out of the can she was holding.

"C'mon, let us see her! Bring her out!"

At first it was just one person. "She's a Bigfoot! She's a freak!" the woman yelled. Then other voices took up the chant. "Bigfoot! Freak!"

Donnetta made a gesture, and then the camera lights bloomed back to life, and people were chanting—"Bring her out! Bring her out! BRING HER OUT!"

Alice felt like her windpipe was narrowing, like she could barely breathe. Lori looked frightened and small, and Phil was scowling as he tugged on his beard. Alice dug her nails into the meat of her palms, hoping—praying—that she'd said the right things and made the right guesses, when Terry, one of the learning guides, stepped through the gates and into the camera's glare.

"You want to see a freak? Take a look, then. I'm a freak." Terry was wearing a gray T-shirt, heavy leather sandals, and a skirt, blue with white polka dots, one of three that Alice knew Taley had made. Terry twirled slowly, then did a little dip. "I got kicked out of my high school for dressing like this. Phil and Lori don't let anyone laugh at me, and I . . ." Terry scowled fiercely at the cameras. "I'm not letting anyone laugh at the kids here."

"I'mb a freak," said Taley, and sniffled, then stepped forward. "I'mb allergic to, like, eberythingd. I can'tb eben be aroundb peanut butter, and my last school voted to be nut-sensitive, but they didn't want to ban anything, so I hadb to dleave. I'm safe heredb," she said, and sniffled. "Doesn'tdb everyone deserved to dbe safe?"

"I'm a freak," said Riya, and stepped forward with her sword. "No one in my family thinks girls should fight. Phil and Lori let me do what I want here. They let me do what I love."

"I'm a freak." Kate was wearing her apron and her hairnet and her heavy black boots. She looked enormous in the camera's lights as she glared at the reporters, big hands balled on her big hips. "Every place I've ever been, people laughed at me. But not here." She raised her head.

"Not here. Not any other girls, either, if I can help it. Not here."

Alice was shaking—her knees, her neck, even her fingertips—but she made herself step forward. She pulled off the vest and mittens and shook out the Mane, like Jessica, and let the light catch its gleam and show herself, all of her, to the world. "That's me in the picture. Some kids played a trick on me. I was swimming and they stole my clothes. I know I'm not little or cute." She could hardly see, with the bright lights burning in her eyes, but she thought she heard murmuring and someone sniffling like they were crying or trying not to. "And my cousin Millie has a glandular condition, which is why she's got hair on her face, but that doesn't make her a monster or a freak! We've got a right to be here, even if we don't look exactly the way we should. People have a right to be . . ."

She sucked in a breath and felt Millie's hands on her shoulders, steadying her.

". . . a right to be who they are and not be afraid," Alice said.

"Maybe we're all freaks," said Taley, who for once was not sniffling. Taley stepped forward, into the light, right in front of Donnetta. For a moment she stood alone. Then she was joined by the boy with the Mohawk.

"I'm a freak," he said in a quiet mumble.

The girl who only wore black—his girlfriend, Alice thought—stepped up beside him and took his hand. "I'm a freak," she said. Her nose stud and cheek piercing glittered in the light. Alice remembered what Taley and Riya told her on her first day at the Center: *Everyone here has something.*

"I'm a freak," said Kelvin Atwater, the boy who did magic.

"I'm a freak," said the girl who loved archery, the boy who played the handmade mandolin, the girl who played football, the boy who liked to tap dance, the girl with two moms and the girl with two dads, the Irish step dancer who'd been kicked out of her high school after her English teacher had intercepted a love note she'd written to her girlfriend, and the star swimmer who'd been kicked out of his house after his parents caught him FaceTiming with his girlfriend, who was a different race than he was.

"I'm a freak," said one person after another, until every learner and guide, even the Steves, were standing shoulder to shoulder, facing the lights. All except Jessica Jarvis, who stood behind Millie, gnawing on one glossy lip and staring at the ground. Millie bared her teeth, and did something to make her fur bristle. Jessica shot Millie a look of pure terror, then stumbled forward as if invisible hands had shoved her.

"I'm a freak," she said. Her voice was practically a whisper. "I have . . . a tail."

Alice gasped. Taley's eyes widened. Riya whipped her head around for a look. *Everyone here has something,* Alice thought again, remembering how Jessica never changed in front of them, how she'd lock the cabin's bathroom and sing "privacy, please!" and how she always wore skirts, never shorts or pants or leggings, even how her bikini had a ruffly skirted bottom.

"It's a very small tail!" Jessica said, and gave a shrill giggle. "But the kids at my last school found out and then they wouldn't leave me alone about it. That's why I came here." She looked at the ground. "Only now I guess the whole world knows."

"Okay, guys." Donnetta Dale raised one slim hand. The cameraman behind her clicked off his lights . . . and then, slowly, the rest of the cameras followed suit. "Look," she said to Lori and Phil. "We're reporters. We got a tip about a story. We had to investigate, but we aren't here to cause any problems. I can see . . ." She paused, straightening her jacket. "I can see we made a mistake. We'll leave you to your evening." She turned toward the van, then stopped, turned around, and looked at the kids and at Alice. "I'd just like to say, personally, that you're all very brave." She waved, and then she was gone.

The crowd started to break up, with people slinking off looking ashamed, leaving a litter of empty cans and wrappers behind them. The remaining news vans packed up and drove away, leaving Lori and Phil, the guides and the learners, and Millie, who hugged Alice fiercely.

"You did it!" Millie cried. "We're safe!"

Taley, who was listening, said, "Who's 'we'?"

Alice and Millie looked at each other. "Well, everyone here, of course," said Alice. "You know, everyone. In general. All of us."

"And me," said Millie. Taley did not seem entirely convinced. "Now they'll leave me alone."

"Congratulations," muttered Jessica Jarvis. She turned toward Alice, looking furious.

"I had friends here!" she snarled. "I was popular! And you . . ." She pointed a manicured finger at Millie. "How'd you even know?"

Millie shrugged modestly. "People like you have a certain smell."

"People with tails?" asked Taley.

"No," said Millie. "Mean ones." She smiled at Jessica.

"I didn't know you had a tail. I just knew you had something."

Jessica looked even more furious. "I'm also very intuitive," Millie continued. "Most Ya—" She stopped herself. Alice held her breath. "Most people in my family are." Jessica muttered three of the seven words that learners at the Center were never allowed to say.

"It's okay," said one of the Steves. "I mean, seriously. I've got a third nipple."

Alice look at him. "You do?"

The Steve lifted his shirt to show her. Alice scrunched up her face. "Ew!"

"Don't hate," said the Steve.

"We're all different," said Taley, her congested voice quiet.

"We're all safe," said Millie . . . and Alice thought, *For now.*

EPILOGUE

O N A COLD, CLEAR MORNING IN DECEMBER, AT the end of a dirt road in a little town called Standish, a twelve-and-a-half-year-old girl named Alice Mayfair stood in the sunshine, wrapped in her wool winter coat, with her curly hair hanging loose against her back. She closed her eyes and listened to the wind sighing through the bare branches, the wavelets lapping at the lake's shore. In the distance, she thought she could hear the sounds of the Yare as they readied their village for winter.

She could smell a dozen different things: wet leaf mulch and the snow that would arrive that night; the curried lentils Kate had served for dinner and the braised tofu she was preparing for the community members who'd still be there for lunch; the freshly cut sod the Yare would use to reinforce the walls of their dugout houses; split logs; and maple syrup boiling in an iron kettle over an open flame.

Millie hadn't brought Alice back to the village—not yet—but she had visited Alice at the Center every day. Together the girls had been making plans, writing lists of what Alice would bring back from New York City and discussing how Millie could visit the No-Fur world and maybe even try out for *The Next Stage*. For the first time in a long time, Alice was excited to go home. It didn't matter that her parents would ignore her, rushing around the apartment, packing for their sojourn in St. Barth's. She wouldn't be ashamed when Felicia rolled her eyes, complaining that Alice had grown out of yet another swimsuit, or wondering out loud how it was possible to gain weight while eating mostly vegetarian.

Alice had a friend. Maybe even friends, plural. She and Taley and Riya had exchanged gifts the night before. Alice had given the other girls jars of lavender honey that Kate had helped her to make. Taley had given her a braided friendship bracelet, and Riya had given her a hand-drawn gift certificate for fencing lessons.

In the quiet of the cold morning, she could hear the rumble of Lee's car as it turned off the main road . . . and the sound of someone running, breathing hard, crunching over frozen leaves and dead branches, coming through the forest. She turned and saw Jeremy Bigelow, the Bigfoot hunter, the boy who'd organized the rally by the lake and put her picture in the newspaper, just as he stepped out of the woods.

Alice squared her shoulders and planted her feet in the dirt, making herself as big and imposing as she could, wishing she had fur that could bristle. "What do you want?"

Jeremy was wearing a bright-blue down jacket that was too big on him and jeans that were slightly too short. His cheeks were pink, and his exhalations came in misty puffs. He bent, catching his breath, then straightened up. "I need to tell you something."

Alice stood, silently waiting.

"But I need to apologize too," said Jeremy. "I know you don't have any reason to believe me, but I wasn't trying to make trouble for you."

"You got a mob to chase me and call me a freak, with three different television stations filming the whole thing," Alice pointed out. Jeremy ducked his head, looking ashamed. Alice half expected him to turn on his heel and vanish back into the woods, but he didn't.

"I know. I'm sorry. I didn't think things would turn out that way. But that isn't what I have to tell you." He shifted from foot to foot. *Stalling,* Alice thought. "The night we had that rally, when you were running, when we thought you were a . . ." He cleared his throat. "You know."

"A Bigfoot," Alice prompted.

Jeremy gave a nod. "Before then, I'd found some of your cousin's, um, hair," he said. "And I guess a strand of your hair was mixed up with it. And then, when you were running, you must have scraped yourself on a stick. My friend Jo found it."

Alice wondered if Jo was the girl in the wheelchair, if she'd been put on clue-gathering duty because she couldn't keep up with the mob.

"Jo is supersmart, and she's hooked into this entire network of people who investigate the paranormal. One of her friends works in a lab in California, and we sent him everything we found. Your hair and the blood."

Alice shrugged, deliberately looking past the boy, toward the gates. A white van cruised slowly along the road that ran parallel to the Center's dirt path. Still no Lee. "So what's the point?" she asked.

Instead of answering, Jeremy pulled a sheet of paper

out of his pocket. "Jo's friend at the lab did this whole analysis."

"And?"

In the quiet, she could hear the click of his throat as he swallowed. "Gary—the guy at the lab—he didn't know what it was. He just knew it wasn't like anything he'd ever seen before."

For a long moment, Alice stood frozen in place. Her tongue felt stiff, and her lips—her entire face—felt numb. She felt shocked . . . except a small part of her wasn't shocked, or even surprised. A small part, it seemed, had been waiting for this news and had known all along that it was coming. "What?" she asked, remembering a joke someone made about her at Miss Pratt's. "Is my blood type 'chocolate'?"

The black Town Car turned the corner, its windshield catching the sun as it came bouncing up the dirt road. "Allie-cat!" called Lee through the opened window. "Merry Christmas!"

"Gary didn't know what the samples were," said Jeremy. "All he knew for sure is that they weren't human." Alice just stared. Jeremy talked faster. "And, listen, the thing you need to know is that there are these people from the government. They knew that Jo and I were looking, and they're probably looking too. I think they were at the rally, and I think they know about"—he waved his hand to encompass the Center and Alice and the lake and maybe even the Yare encampment, miles across the water—"all of this." He gave Alice a steady look as Alice wondered exactly how much he knew. "I came here to warn you. You need to be careful."

"But what am I?" Alice whispered as Lee got out of the car in his black jacket and black cap, and started loading her luggage into the trunk. Jeremy didn't answer. Alice stood there, frozen in place, watching as he melted back into the woods and disappeared.

ACKNOWLEDGMENTS

I MUST BEGIN BY THANKING MY YOUNGER daughter, Phoebe, whose interest in Bigfoots sparked my own. When she was six, Phoebe was obsessed with a show on Animal Planet called *Finding Bigfoot*, where a pack of professional Bigfoot hunters traveled the world in search of evidence that the legendary creatures were real. Phoebe got me thinking about Bigfoots . . . about what they'd be like, why they'd hide, and why one of them might want desperately to join the "No-Fur" world.

Phoebe was my "test kid," or my "keditor," listening to each draft of this story, telling me whether or not kids would know a certain word or TV show, or think a joke was funny. I was so lucky to have her help. Plus, she's just great company. Thanks, Phoebe . . . you'll always be one of my very favorite No-Furs!

Special shout-outs to Phoebe's teachers Ben Warrington and Adenike Walker at The Philadelphia School, and her classmates in Primary Unit D, who sat through so many versions of this story, listening raptly when they were into it, squirming when they weren't, and asking when they could buy the book for real. Primary D, please know I am very grateful for your patience; I tried to take out all the squirmy bits, and the answer to "when" is "now."

My daughter Lucy had an idea for a story about a convention for hidden creatures, who would gather at a summer camp each year and enjoy activities like buffet meals, Zumba classes, and seminars on how to avoid humans. Lu, I'm sorry if I borrowed your idea and twisted it until it became this story . . . and if I used your experiences at a certain summer camp that will remain forever anonymous to make the Experimental Center for Love and Learning—where they won't tolerate intolerance.

Thanks to Aimee Friedman, whose encouragement was invaluable as she listened to the very first description of this story, read an early draft of this book, and told me I had an actual children's story.

My agent, Joanna Pulcini, was, as always, invaluable for her help and insightful feedback in helping Millie, Alice, and Jeremy feel like real people on the page.

Writing for children was a new adventure for me, and I was lucky enough to have the support and expertise of a fantastic crew of professionals at Aladdin. My editor, Amy Cloud (isn't that the best name ever for a children's book editor?), was Alice and Millie's most enthusiastic fan and supporter, and was as nice as could be when she told me that some of the words you can use in adult books you can't use in books for children.

If you're as impressed as I am with how beautiful this book is, thank Jihyuk Kim, who did the gorgeous jacket illustration; Sara Mulvanny, who did the beautiful map and interior illustrations; and designer Laura Lyn DiSiena.

Thanks to Jon Anderson, the president of the Simon & Schuster Children's Publishing Division, and Mara Anastas, the publisher of Aladdin, for their enthusiasm and support. Thanks also to deputy publisher Mary Marotta; editorial director Fiona Simpson; Lucille Rettino and her associates Carolyn Swerdloff and Matt Pantoliano in marketing; Jennifer Romanello and Jodie Hockensmith in publicity; the brilliant sales team: Michael Selleck, Gary Urda, Josh Wood, Christina Pecorale, John Hardy, Jerry Jensen,

Victor Iannone, Karen Lahey, Danielle Esposito, and Lorelei Kelly; Stephanie Voros and Deane Norton in subsidiary rights; managing editor Katherine Devendorf; and last but absolutely not least, Stephanie Evans Biggins, copy editor, and Tom Finnegan, proofreader.

Thanks to the home team—Terri Gottlieb, who helps with kids, food, and gardening (all of the important stuff); Meghan Burnett, who is, hands down, the best assistant in the world; my mom, Fran; sister, Molly; and brothers, Jake and Joe.

And, finally, to my husband, Bill Syken, who walked with me on the boardwalk in Ventnor, helped me figure out what kind of adventures two kids and a little Bigfoot could get into, and was endlessly patient when I was off in the neighborhood of make-believe: all of my thanks and love.